THE GODDESS OF

GREEN LAKE

CONSTANCE SPRAGUE

SILVER BEECH PRESS

The Goddess of Green Lake
Second Edition

10 9 8 7 6 5 4 3 2

ISBN-13: 978-0998191508
ISBN-10: 0998191507

For Mike McCuddin, who knows where the otters are.

CHAPTER ONE

Eel sat up with a gasp, sucking in air. In the silence blanketing the dark room his pulse beat in his ears like a drum. A foghorn moaned across the bay. He rolled over on the couch and tried to recall the song that had pulled him from his dream. All that remained in his mind was a girl's voice, haunting, irresistible.

He listened for any sound from upstairs before grabbing his leather jacket and slipping out the back door. Fergus was sitting at the top of the steps.

Something was scurrying around on the lawn.

"He gets restless in the house," Fergus whispered.

At the sound of Fergus's voice Shredney darted up to sniff Eel.

"Hey buddy," Eel said, ruffling the little creature's leafy coat. Shredney brushed up against Fergus's shin and tilted his head inquisitively.

"It's all right, Shred. We're not going anywhere," Fergus said.

Shredney scampered into the shadowy moonlight. Watching him, Eel lit a cigarette and said, "Do you ever wish you could go back?"

"Where?"

"The other side. The place you came from, wherever it is."

"No." Fergus stared out into the small backyard. "This is where I belong now. With Alice. And our children."

Eel raised an eyebrow.

"Another's on the way," Fergus said.

"Good for you." The moonlight slipped behind a tree. "I've got to find another place to be."

"You can stay here as long as you like."

"Nah. 'S been nice. Seein' you and Alice. And the baby. But..."

"Where will you go?"

"North. Maybe Portland. Seattle. Music scene might be better for me."

"You have a plan?"

"Mitch and Natalie have friends up there."

"Are you all right?"

Eel peered at the older man. "Did you ever wake up with a song stuck in your head? A song you never heard before?"

Fergus eyed him carefully. "The siren's song."

Silence pooled in the stillness. "Just feel like I've got to go up there. Can't explain it."

Fergus nodded. "I've always wanted to see the great forest there." He smiled slightly. "They say you can take the Green Man out of the tree, but you can't take the tree out of the Green Man."

Eel gave him a look. "Did you just make that up?"

"Old saying. On the other side."

"Want to come along?"

Fergus shrugged. "Maybe in the summer we can drive up the redwood highway. Tommy and Abby are coming to visit after they graduate. He'd like to see you."

"That'd be great. By then maybe I'll have something going on."

Fergus stretched and stood up. "Sounds like a plan. I better get some sleep." He went inside.

Eel lingered in the moonlight, watching Shredney skittering around, sniffing the lawn and snapping at bugs, looking for all the world like any ordinary dog. Eel lit another cigarette and considered the disappointments of the past two months. Lackluster gigs and open mic nights, feeling out of sync with the music he heard in clubs and bars. Aside from Mitch and Natalie, he hadn't found any friends on his wave length.

Being around Alice and Fergus had given him the opportunity to see, for the first time in his life, what happiness might look like. In their little bungalow, with the new baby and their new lives, Alice and Fergus appeared to have reached some golden plateau. Eel envied the way they worked as a team, dealing with the ups and downs of life. And envy was new to him.

~ ~ ~

Callie took off her shoes and tied them to her backpack when she got to the beach at Fort Ebey. The water was freezing cold, yet she wanted to feel it on her bare feet.

The Sound was calm this morning. Seagulls wheeled across the gray sky. A handful of seaweed gatherers worked their way over the stones at the water's edge. In the distance a ferry churned smoothly toward the San Juans. Callie walked down the beach, enjoying the sea scent. She let Rugby off his leash and watched him tear down the pebbles toward a pile of brown flotsam. The little dog stopped beside the pile and started barking at it.

"Rugby!" Callie shouted, running toward him. "Rugby! Get away!"

Her heart sank as she got close enough to see that the body lying much too still was a sea otter. She edged closer and saw something move in the otter's thick brown fur. The baby was pressed close to its mother's belly, clutching her fur in its tiny paw. Perhaps sensing Callie, it looked up and fixed her with a stare.

Kneeling, Callie whispered, "Hi, baby. What are you doing here? You all alone now?"

She held completely still. The baby kept staring at her. In its unblinking gaze Callie detected something more than animal cunning, as if the tiny otter were assessing her. Rugby bounded closer with another bark, and the baby tried to burrow under its dead mother.

"Rugby! Sit!" Callie waited until the dog settled on its haunches before she turned back to the otter. A pool of dark blood had soaked into the sand around the mother's head. Sea otters didn't normally venture into the Sound. She wondered what had driven this one so far from the ocean. The pup couldn't be more than eight weeks old. Too young to survive alone.

The pup wriggled out from under its mother and put a paw on Callie's knee. A shiver ran up her arms. "Okay, kid," she muttered. "You're going to have to trust me, okay?" She grabbed him by the scruff of his neck as if he were a cat. He didn't struggle or take his eyes off her.

She pulled her sweatshirt out of her backpack and wrapped him in it, cradling him in her arms. She wouldn't be able to care for the baby herself, but she knew a place that could. "Now the question is, are you going to behave in the car?"

She strapped him against her lap with the seatbelt. The baby seemed to accept the situation and fell asleep as she drove to The Sounding.

It was harder than she expected to turn over the pup. The baby seemed reluctant to let Callie of his sight, even after she brought him to the edge of the otter pool. He sniffed the concrete and shook his head. He kept turning back to Callie after she put him down, reaching for her with his paw. Finally two older otters came closer, and the baby dove in and swam to them.

Callie's throat constricted, as if she were saying goodbye forever to a close friend. She hid her unexpected rush of emotion from the aquarium staff.

They assured her that she was doing the right thing. They were optimistic about the pup's chances. They had an experienced female sea otter who they hoped would teach the baby how to take care of himself.

They asked Callie if she wanted to give the pup a name. She said she would like to wait and see how the pup developed before choosing a name. She didn't say that she wanted to make sure he lived.

On the drive home she tried to tell herself the baby would be fine, even though history suggested otherwise. Sea otters in the Sound had been hunted nearly to extinction by the time they finally received federal protection in 1911. The small population of sea otters currently living off the coast of Washington had been brought down from Alaskan waters in the early 1970s in an effort to reestablish them in the region that had once been their playground. With their numbers so diminished, every one was precious, but Callie was surprised by the urgency she felt for this pup. She couldn't forget the way he had nestled in her arms. Although she had tried to be cool and professional at the aquarium, now, alone with her sleeping dog, Callie couldn't deny the eerie feeling that the pup was somehow meant for her. Weirder still, she was sure the pup felt the same way.

As she arrived home, she mumbled to herself, "It's a wild animal. It doesn't care about you."

Rugby tumbled out of the car, wagging his tail. "Not like you, huh, buddy? You love me, dontcha?" she said.

"You really need a new boyfriend." Celeste was leaning against the garage door, an affectionate smirk on her face.

"I don't need a boyfriend," Callie said, bustling past.

In the kitchen, Viola, the oldest of the sisters, looked up from peeling potatoes and said, "I told Ernie we'd be at the hall by eight."

Callie paused on her way through the room. "Are we practicing tonight?"

"You forgot?" Viola's pale blue eyes searched Callie's face for signs of levity.

Callie shook her head. "No. I mean, yeah, I kind of forgot. I got distracted at the beach."

"Oooh. Sounds promising. What's he like?" Celeste plopped into a chair with a grin.

Callie made a face. "You're the one who needs a boyfriend."

Celeste started twisting a lock of hair in her fingers. "It's not like you to forget a rehearsal."

Callie bit her lip. "Okay. You got me. He's got silky brown hair and the cutest eyes, and I think he likes me."

"Hah! I knew it!" Celeste crowed.

"And he's a sea otter."

Viola said, "Really?"

"Really. A baby. I found him on the beach. I took him to the aquarium."

"Huh," Celeste grunted. "You couldn't have found a nice merman?"

"Let's not go there," Viola murmured.

Celeste stopped smiling and shot a look at Viola. She dipped her chin and said, "Seriously, that's great you rescued an otter. For all the good it'll do."

"Oh come on! Do you have to be so negative?" Callie said.

"Hey! You don't want me to make jokes. You don't want me to talk about your love life. You're cramping my style. You know that?"

Callie rolled her eyes. It was no use being mad at Celeste. With her wild blonde curls and dazzling smile, she was like some irrepressible, sexy angel. She had no interest in finding Mr. Right, but she thoroughly enjoyed the process of hunting Mr. Right Now.

"Sorry Cele. The baby was just so cute. And so helpless. You know?"

"Yeah. I know. Not my type. By the way, your manly man called three times this afternoon."

"Haven?"

"Yeah, him. What kind of a name is that, anyway? He sounded all in a snit about some meeting you're supposed to go to."

Callie frowned. "Right. I'll call him." She started out of the room.

"You can't go tonight. We've only got three weeks until opening night."

"I know." The stairs creaked as Callie went up to the room she'd lived in all her life. When her grandparents had moved into a smaller, one-story house a few blocks away, she finally had the room all to herself, her sisters having spread into the other bedrooms. Callie loved the old bungalow with its deep porch and mullioned windows. On clear days she could see the light glinting off Salmon Bay.

When she tried to return Haven's calls, she got his voice mail and left a short message. She would go to the next meeting. But she didn't want to talk about it now, or listen to Haven talk about it. She felt strangely uneasy. She needed time to settle the waves, to find her serene center, before the rehearsal.

She lay on her bed and thought about the baby otter. She couldn't get over the feeling that he had reached out for her—had somehow found her—for a reason. She wouldn't dream of trying to explain that to her sisters. They didn't have much patience with her mermaid theories. But she couldn't stop thinking about it, wondering how he was doing in his artificial home. Would he be floating on his back, enjoying a little snooze? She thought of the way sea otters can sleep riding the waves in the ocean, linking together and anchoring themselves with strands of kelp to form a living raft. She closed her eyes and imagined herself bobbing gently up and down on the sea, surrounded by softly humming otters.

"Hey! Rise and shine Calypso gal! It's time to go!"

Callie opened her eyes. Celeste was standing over her.

"Okay, okay. I'm coming," she said, sitting up groggily. "Can I eat something first?"

"You can eat in the car."

As they went out the door, Callie mumbled, "I wonder if I could eat floating on my back in the water."

Viola turned around and looked at her. "Are you okay?"

"Yeah. I'm okay. I'm not an otter."

Viola and Celeste exchanged a glance.

"Okaaay," said Celeste. "That's one thing we can agree on."

CHAPTER TWO

When she heard the splash, Callie turned toward the sound, muffled in the dense fog that covered the lake. A splash that loud usually meant some tourist had fallen in. In her years of rowing around Green Lake, Callie had developed a personal radar that distinguished between sounds of distress and sounds of high spirits. She understood the language of the lake itself—the gentle swish and murmur of the water, the honking ducks and skittering coots, the wind's breath upon the shore brush.

But this late-afternoon splash had the distinctive signature of a disgruntled human—the slap of palms against the surface, underscored by a discontented muttering. Callie waited, her hands resting on the oars. Would the hapless boater be rescued by his own party or left to flail? When a ringing "Very funny!" ripped through the cottony mist, she began to row.

He was thrashing across the water. Had he been a more graceful swimmer, he might have been mistaken for a seal, a trick of the water gleaming on his black leather jacket and the mop of green dreadlocks swirling about his head like seaweed.

Raising her chin so her voice would carry, she said, "Can I give you a lift?"

He looked at her, and Callie paused with the oars in midstroke, until she noticed that he had also paused in his efforts to tread water, and he was definitely sinking.

"Here, let me help you," she said, rowing closer. As the boat came near, he grabbed the side and struggled to climb in. He was skinny and pale. Callie guessed that his wet clothes weighed more than he did. When he had managed to fling one boot-clad foot over the edge, he got stuck, unable to drag the other boot out of the water. She locked the oars and stepped over to pull him into the boat. Reaching across his back she got a grip on his jacket. For a moment they teetered together on the edge, then she fell backwards onto the floor with him on top of her.

"Sorry," he said, quickly rolling off.

"Don't worry. Happens all the time," she said, getting up and resuming her seat by the oars.

He sat in the bow. Sizing him up, Callie guessed he was either a student or a tourist.

"It's a little early in the season for swimming," she said.

"Wasn't my idea," he replied. He patted his jacket pocket and pulled out a sodden pack of cigarettes. He grimaced and tossed them into the lake.

"Hey! What are you doing?" Callie stopped rowing and glared at him.

He shrugged. "What?"

"I can't believe you just did that. Maybe you should go back in the water too."

He frowned. "Hey. I'm sorry, all right?"

"No. It's not all right." She looked at the pack of cigarettes drifting out of reach. "You pick those back up, or you can get out now."

He hesitated, then leaned out and grabbed the pack from the water. He settled back on the seat and held the pack toward Callie. "Want one?" he asked.

"What do you think?" she said.

He said nothing, and Callie tried to concentrate on getting him to shore. She couldn't help noticing that his eyes were a vivid shade of green.

"So, what do you do?" she asked briskly.

"I'm a musician."

"Oh."

"You don't like music?"

"Of course I like music. Let me guess. You don't play violin."

He was watching her intently, but he said nothing.

"Or bassoon," she continued.

"What's your point?"

"Nothing."

He stared at her flatly. "Nothing?"

Callie sat up straighter. "That's what I said."

He looked at the fast-approaching shore. "You've got it all figured out, haven't you?"

"Maybe. Maybe you're some wannabe in a leather jacket who came to Seattle to make it big in the music scene and add to his collection of groupies."

"You think I have a collection? And that'd be wrong, in your opinion?"

"You don't care about my opinion."

"D'you wish I did?"

Callie gripped the oars tighter. "Listen, I don't care who you are or what you do. I happen to think that music is a gift, and it should be used for the greater good, not for personal gain."

"Lighten up."

"Oh, I will, as soon as you get out of my boat."

He stood up. "Don't let me stop you. Thanks for the lift." He jumped out and began wading to the shore.

Callie watched him disappear into the fog. But long after she had tied up the boat and walked back to her bike, she remembered those startling green eyes.

Eel trudged across the sodden grass, replaying the scene in his head. Since moving to Seattle, he had learned to accept wetness as the default state of normal. But as the waters of Green Lake had closed over his head, he couldn't help feeling that there ought to be a limit.

A sudden swerve by the paddleboat while he was standing up in the back had precipitated his plunge into the cold water. He'd heard Mitch and Natalie laughing as he went under. Seconds later when he bobbed to the surface, the paddleboat had already drifted out of sight. Somewhere in the rapidly thickening mist he had heard a dog barking.

The fog had completely shrouded the paddleboat. He heard Mitch calling, telling him to swim to the boat, but Eel's sense of direction was out of whack, and his ability to tread water severely hampered by his heavy boots. He had to concentrate to keep his head above water and didn't relish a game of Marco Polo.

He heard the barking dog again. It sounded a lot closer, and out of the mist a rowboat emerged with a small black and white dog standing in the bow.

"Can I give you a lift?"

It was a musical voice, and it echoed deep in Eel's brain like the memory of a long lost lover. Sitting behind the dog was a girl with oars in her hands. The mist shimmered about her, almost as if she had materialized from it. In the instant before he replied, he took note of her long, wavy blonde hair, pale as the mist, and her large, gray eyes, liquid as the lake.

After he had clambered awkwardly into the boat, he had hoped to strike up a warm friendship with this goddess, but the first flame sputtered when he tossed his cigarettes in the lake. Looking back on it now, he could see that it wasn't a smooth move, even if he was chilled to the bone and not thinking as clearly as he might have.

As he squelched back to his car, he clenched his teeth and wondered if he could afford another pack. He pulled out his sodden wallet. A quick check revealed one five and two ones—the sum of his assets after months of one-night stands and dead-end gigs. He looked down the street for someplace to buy cigarettes.

"Hey! What happened to you? Thought you drowned, man." Mitch came up beside him, and punched his arm. "Jeez, you're drenched."

"We tried to find you. Did you swim all the way back?" Natalie asked.

Eel shrugged. "Yeah. Going to get some smokes."

"You still want to head over to Fremont to meet that drummer?" Mitch asked.

Eel considered mentioning the girl who had rescued him, but he didn't want to listen to Mitch and Natalie asking a bunch of questions. "Gonna call it a night," he said. "You go meet the guy if you want. I gotta get a new plan."

The street lamps came on. Reflections shone on the pavement. Eel trudged under a dark sky from which a light drizzle was falling. After the cold lake, the rain felt almost warm on his skin.

He tramped along the damp gravel path to his car. The prints left by his boots glinted darkly in the streetlights, turning from gray to green as moss sprang to life in his footsteps.

CHAPTER THREE

Eel leaned back in the chair, watching the frown lines deepen on the administrator's face. He clenched his teeth and waited for the rejection.

The woman across the desk looked up at him and said, "Mr. MacGregor, quite frankly, I don't see anything in this application that indicates you're suited for this kind of work."

Eel exhaled slowly. "Right. Guess I shoulda gone to janitor school."

The woman shifted in her chair and cleared her throat. "It's not that it's a difficult job, but I wonder if it's something you really want to do." She stared at Eel as if waiting for him to recognize how out of place he looked with his black leather and chains in this room filled with bright posters of sea creatures and upbeat environmental slogans.

Eel leaned forward and clasped his hands together. "Listen, I just need a job. Any job. Any job where I don't have to wear a tie and sit at a desk or sell something." He paused and glanced out the window at Elliott Bay. "'S nice here. I can push a broom. Wash windows. Whatever. What's the problem?"

The woman pursed her lips. "There's no problem, per se, Mr. MacGregor—"

"Name's Eel."

"Sorry?"

"My name. 'S Eel."

"Well, Seal—"

Eel suppressed a smile. "Eel," he said slowly.

"Oh. I see. Well... Eel, the thing is, we've had a lot of turnover in this position, and we're looking for someone who will stay on for at least a year. We'd like to have some continuity."

"That's me then. I'm not going anywhere. God knows." He looked directly at the administrator. "S'how about it? Gimme a chance."

While the woman stared at his application, Eel fumed silently. His dreams of rock and roll success had come to this: pleading for a day job as a janitor at a glorified fish tank. He had half a mind to walk out, but he had nowhere to go and less than five dollars in his pocket.

"All right then. Let me show you around. Could you start tomorrow?"

A weight rolled off his chest. "Yeah. I can do that."

To his surprise, Eel found that the job at the aquarium wasn't half-bad. The work itself wasn't taxing, though it took him a while to get used to the idea of wearing the green janitor jumpsuit. But even the worst part, cleaning the toilets, didn't seem that bad compared to what some of the volunteers had to do. He didn't envy the ones who strapped on scuba gear and cleaned the inside of the tanks, for instance. He was able to take frequent breaks outside on the walkways that ran between the harbor-seal tanks and the bay, and he felt at home in the relative darkness of the indoor space. He enjoyed seeing the fish swimming around him while he vacuumed the underground observation areas. And people left him alone, which suited him just fine.

Most of all, he liked watching the otters that slipped and flipped in and out of the water all day long in the pools above. Eel hadn't expected to encounter any furry creatures in an aquarium, and the boundless energy and goofy antics of the otters completely won him over. He marveled at the way they seemed in a perpetual good mood, in spite of being confined to their limited quarters.

And when, halfway through his first week, Eel noticed the tiniest otter of them all, he was mesmerized.

"Isn't he the cutest ever?"

The girl had pink cheeks and dark brown eyes, her hair pulled back in a ponytail. Eel grunted noncommittally. When his silence didn't stop her from babbling on about the baby otter, he listened and learned that the otter was an orphan, and that its survival was something of a miracle. But when the girl started asking him questions about himself, he said he had to get back to work.

From then on, Eel made a point of keeping an eye on the baby otter. Somehow the time spent watching the sea otters provided a kind of antidote to the soul-crushing disappointment and failure of his music career. Though he still believed in his own talent, he wasn't having much success breaking into the Seattle scene.

He was staring at the otters, musing on the chances of getting hired for a steady playing gig, when the hairs on the back of his neck stood up, and he felt an odd prickling in his skin. He sneaked a look over his shoulder and sucked in his breath. She was watching the otters too, completely unaware of his presence. Eel stared at her, his hands suddenly sweating, his mouth dry. When she glanced over at him, he saw the surprise in her face. Her mouth dropped open as she eyed his uniform.

"You work here?" The scorn in her tone did nothing to raise his hopes that the passage of time had softened her opinion of him.

He nodded. She shook her head in a disbelieving way. "I never expected to see someone like you here," she said.

"What's that supposed to mean?"

She sniffed and turned to watch the otters. "Most people who work here care passionately about the environment."

"That's what you're passionate about, huh?"

"Of course. Any thinking person knows that's the most important issue in the world right now."

Eel lifted an eyebrow. "Tell that to the starving people in Africa."

"They're starving because of the environment."

"Oh? Not because Johnny America wants to buy his girl a diamond ring and doesn't care whose blood plays for it?"

Callie faltered. "Well, yes. That's true. Greed is the root of the problem."

Eel nodded. "All right, then. We agree on something."

They watched the otters in silence for several minutes until the baby otter swam near the glass and did a complete flip right in front of Callie. Then he made a funny noise and looked at her as he paddled backward across the pool.

"He seems to like you," said Eel.

"He's my baby."

"I can see the resemblance."

"What do you mean?" She frowned at him uncertainly.

"He's cute."

"Oh." Without meaning to, Callie started talking. She told Eel how she had found the baby and brought him in, and that she had been trying to decide on a name for him. Eel held completely still as he listened. He wanted to ask her name, but he didn't want to scare her away. He kept his hands in his pockets and tried to sound relaxed as he prompted her to talk more about the otter.

She finally turned to go and said, "I need to find the trainers and tell them what his name is."

"What's it gonna be?"

She studied his face, as if reading a warning label.

"Come on. You can tell me," he said.

She shook her head. "I think I should tell them first. I mean," she shrugged, "what do you care?"

"Why wouldn't I care? The little guy? He likes me too."

"Oh really? What makes you think that?"

17

"He always comes over when I'm here. Gives me a wink. I can tell. He likes me."

She laughed softly. "Oh you think so, huh?"

"What? You think I'm making it up?"

"No. I think you're probably so deluded that you honestly believe it. You're a musician."

"Fine," Eel said. "Think what you want. What do you know about musicians anyway?"

At this Callie laughed, smiled broadly and started walking away. "See you around," she said.

Watching her disappear, Eel fought the urge to go after her. He turned back to the otters and noticed the baby swimming tight circles in front of him. When the baby saw him, it winked and dove under the water, leaving Eel more perplexed than ever. After the girl's skeptical dismissal, he didn't know whether to believe what he had just seen or not. But there was no way he could forget it. Or her.

CHAPTER FOUR

From the back of the hall Callie listened to Haven delivering one of his go-get-em speeches. Even though she had watched him do this dozens of times, it never failed to kindle her hope of a greener future. Day after day in class, her instructors bludgeoned the students with brutal statistics about environmental degradation and habitat loss. The too-little-too-late efforts of the world's conservation groups were no match for the relentless corporate attack.

But here, surrounded by a motley assembly of peaceable nature lovers in an out-of-the-way auditorium in Lake City, it was possible to surrender to the soothing rhetoric of resistance, renewal, and restoration, and to believe the damage could be undone. As she felt her nerves unwinding, Callie gazed at Haven, admiring again his strong jaw and broad shoulders, the clear light in his eyes. Seeing the crowd respond to the persuasive urgency in his voice, she felt a glow of pride.

Afterward, when the audience was trickling out of the room, Haven remained in the center of a small knot of the faithful and answered follow-up questions. Callie stood back, waiting as usual. He caught her eye and gave her a quick smile, shrugging his shoulders as if to say, what could he do? When the last eager activist had turned to the door, he came over and said, "Well, what'd you think?"

"I thought it went well," she replied.

He nodded. "Yes. It went well. I don't think many of them are going to show up for the protest though. They didn't seem angry enough."

"Maybe they're saving their anger for the protest."

"I hope so." They walked out of the building together. The evening air was cool. Callie zipped up her hoodie. A group of students passed them on the sidewalk, laughing and talking. One of the boys had his arm around a girl, and they walked behind the rest with a kind of rhythm of their own. Callie glanced up at Haven, his arms laden with boxes of pamphlets. He was rattling on about the upcoming protest against allowing more cruise ships in Puget Sound. It was a really important issue, but there were times when Callie wondered if she would ever mean as much to Haven as the next protest.

She listened while he went over details of the usual logistical planning that consumed his thoughts. When they reached their bikes, she bit her lip and waited for him to ask her about her day. He strapped the boxes to his bike rack and was fastening his helmet when he finally looked at her and said, "So, anything new with you?"

She hadn't told him about the baby otter. She had been waiting for a chance to tell him the whole story. But when she looked at Haven sitting on his bike, ready to go, she decided it could wait. He had more important things on his mind.

"Nope," she replied, hopping onto her own bike.

As they rode off on the Burke–Gilman trail toward Haven's apartment, Callie told herself it was perfectly normal not to mention the baby otter. Yet even as she thought this, a vision of Eel's acid green eyes rose in her mind, and she briefly swerved into the gravel.

It was nearly midnight when she arrived back at the house. She heard music coming from the kitchen. Her sisters would be baking cookies for the final dress rehearsal the next night.

"Calypso Gal! We were just talking about you," Celeste said. "Vi thought you might be spending the night at Safe Haven's, but I told her you'd be home, like the good girl you are. I'm guessing ole Have has to save his energy for the big protest, right?"

Callie slipped off her jacket and sat down at the kitchen table, where a plate of warm cookies gave off an aroma of cinnamon and peanut butter. "What kind of cookies are these?"

"Try one. Tell me what you think," said Viola, pulling another tray from the oven.

Callie bit into one and chewed for a minute. "Are you going for weird? Because that's what I'm tasting."

"Okay. Weird. But, good weird? Or inedible weird?" asked Viola.

Callie shrugged. "I guess it would depend on how hungry you were."

"How 'bout that they're free?" Celeste added.

Callie finished the cookie and looked up at the clock on the wall.

"Hey, I'm sorry. I didn't mean to get home so late. I know we were going to practice."

Viola turned off the oven, put down her potholder, and smiled sweetly. "We still are."

"Now?" said Callie. "I'm so tired."

"What's the matter. Did your big strong boyfriend wear you out?" said Celeste.

Callie grimaced. "Of course not."

"Of course not!" hooted Celeste. "Well, great. Then there's no reason we can't run through the set one time before you go off to dream sweet dreams of your sexy guy."

"Oh cut it out. I know you think Haven's boring. Just because he doesn't wear leather pants and play drums. You know, being cool is over-rated. I'd much rather have a guy who cares about the things that matter than some jerk who only thinks about where to put his next tattoo."

"Whoa. I think we hit a nerve," said Celeste, lifting her eyebrows at Viola.

Viola sighed and took Callie by the elbow, steering her gently toward the upright piano in the living room. "Come on, Callie. The sooner we run through these songs, the sooner you can go to sleep."

"Fine." Callie tried to ignore Celeste's taunting. It's not like it was the first time her sister had criticized Haven. But, Callie reflected uneasily, it was the first time that her sister's gibes had echoed a murmur of discontent in her own heart.

While Viola arranged the sheet music, Celeste put an arm around Callie's shoulders and said in a gentler tone, "Hey, Cal. Just kidding, you know? I like ole Haven. It's not his fault if he's about as exciting as a bran muffin. Not everybody can be Johnny Depp. And Haven, you know? He's a regular guy."

Celeste laughed as she said this, and Callie had to fight not to smile. She really shouldn't laugh at Haven, she told herself.

CHAPTER FIVE

Two nights later, in the cool drizzle of an early-April evening, Eel eyed the crowd waiting in line and felt oddly discomfited by the realization that he didn't stand out at all. Although there were plenty of the usual Seattle types—swathed in a palette of earthy Patagonia shades and Gore-Tex—they were outnumbered by the more free-spirited Fremont characters whose style defied classification. Hairstyles ranged the rainbow, and the fashion focus was a kaleidoscopic spin from retro hippies to New Wave punk, with a smattering of zany originals. Back in Virginia, Eel's green Mohawk, black leather, and gritty demeanor had been enough to get the attention of locals. But here, he was just another oddball in the crowd. He wasn't sure if he liked it.

When a man on stilts wearing an Abe Lincoln-style beard and bright orange dreadlocks handed him a flyer, Eel expected to read about some upcoming concert. But the flyer was an invitation to become part of the show in the next season. Eel stuffed it in his back pocket and turned to Mitch and Natalie.

"What's this thing called again?" he asked, pulling out a cigarette.

"The LIP Festival," Natalie said.

"Lip?"

"Stands for Let It Pour. It's all about rain here, I guess. Carmen says it's music and jokes and stuff. And beer." Natalie grinned at Mitch as she said this.

Eel watched a woman walk by in fishnet stockings, stiletto heels, and a tight red satin strapless dress.

"You reckon she's in the show?" he asked Natalie, who had convinced him to join her and Mitch tonight.

"Maybe. Carmen says it's pretty wild. Kind of like burlesque used to be, she said. I don't know what that means, but Carmen's fun. If she says it'll be fun, it'll be fun," said Natalie, whose hand was tucked in Mitch's jacket pocket for warmth.

The line began to move. Eel stubbed out his cigarette. "What's she do, then? Sing?"

"I don't think so. Something to do with ropes."

They shuffled through the entrance into a cavernous dark room packed with people. A low roar of conversation surrounded them. They found three folding chairs together near the back and sat down.

Mitch went to get in line for drinks. Eel opened the program and read the list of acts, grunting skeptically at the mention of a juggler and a magician. But when Mitch returned with the beer, Eel found that to his liking. He leaned back, prepared to watch whatever it was that Seattle considered entertainment.

The lights went down, and a drum roll commenced, followed by a crash of cymbals and a thudding beat. All heads turned to see a procession moving slowly up the aisle. Six large men, clothed in flowing robes and ceremonial headdresses, marched gravely to the rhythm of a bass drum, which stopped abruptly after they had spread out across the stage, facing the audience. There was a moment of dramatic silence. Then the center figure shouted a command and all the men dropped their robes, revealing beer guts of various sizes, bulging above generous loin cloths. While swinging short ropes with balls attached to the ends, they chanted, "We're boys, with pois. We're big boys, with pois."

The audience howled with laughter, and cheered wildly at the end when the men burst their water-balloon pois.

Natalie and Mitch giggled like little kids. Eel took a large gulp of beer. Okay, he thought. It could be worse.

The next few acts included a comedian, a hoop artist, and a quirky guitar player. Eel had finished his beer and was beginning to fidget, eyeing the exits, when the lighting shifted to a smoldering red hue, and Natalie whispered, "Here comes Carmen."

The stage musicians began to play a sultry song, while a singer in a slinky, black dress sang suggestive lyrics. Spotlights swooped over the audience, lighting up scantily clad women positioned in the aisles. Heavy ropes dropped down beside them from the ceiling.

"Please welcome the Rock-a-Bye Babes!" said the MC.

The women hoisted themselves on the ropes, writhing upward with bumps and grinds synchronized with the music. Eel watched spellbound as the limber young women twirled, kicked, and struck breathtaking poses, many of them upside down, all the while with expressions of erotic detachment that made him squirm.

The act ended in a flourish of seemingly perilous sudden drops. Eel applauded enthusiastically with the rest of the audience as the Babes sashayed out of sight. He leaned over and asked Natalie, "Which one was your friend?"

"She was the one up by the stage, in this row."

"'S a good act," said Eel, nodding approvingly.

"Yeah. She's incredibly fit."

"Guess you'd have to be."

Eel was about to ask if Carmen had a boyfriend, when the lighting changed again. The room went dark but for a single warm spotlight on center stage, and Eel completely forgot what he was going to say as three women in silvery blue gowns stepped into the light. There she was, in the middle, glowing like some unearthly spirit.

The room fell silent, and the women began to sing, a cappella. Their voices wove in and around each other, their lines of harmony and melody floating with the fluid beauty of a mountain stream. But it was her voice that called him. He'd heard it before in a dream.

He stared with hungry eyes. The two women beside her were beautiful, no question—one taller, with the same blonde hair cut short, like a punk pixie, the other somewhat rounder of face and form, but with a resemblance strong enough that Eel guessed they were sisters. He considered looking in the program to see, but he couldn't take his eyes off her.

When the song ended, she introduced the group as the Droplettes and joked about their next song, which they had also written. It was a syncopated blues, bawdy and sweet at the same time. Eel was sweating in his seat. Every time they came to the refrain, which had something to do with getting wet, there were whistles and groans of appreciation from the crowd, and when the trio finished, a number of men in the audience gave them a standing ovation. Eel would have joined them, but he needed a moment to regain his composure.

The rest of the show went by in a blur. When the lights finally came up, he looked through the program, but it didn't list the individual names of The Droplettes. He wanted to find her, to tell her how great she was, even though she probably wouldn't care what he thought. He hadn't forgotten her disdain in their previous meetings.

He left Mitch and Natalie and worked his way to the side of the stage. Several of the performers were hanging around, but he didn't see her. He tried to get closer, until a bear-sized guy in a striped suit barred his way with a curt, "Performers only past here."

Eel was wondering if he could talk his way past, when one of the Babes walked by. He caught her arm and said, "'Scuse me? I need to talk to one of the singers. The Droplettes? D'you know where they are?"

The woman grinned at him slyly and looked him up and down before she answered. "They already left. But you can talk to me if you like."

Eel shook his head. "Thanks, but I have to talk to one of them."

The woman's expression altered slightly. "The blonde with the hair and the attitude?"

Eel looked at her blankly.

The woman shrugged. "They work at a Swedish bakery in Ballard. You might find them there."

"Thanks. Thanks a lot," Eel said, turning to go.

The woman grabbed his elbow and said, "If you don't find what you need with them... I'm a good listener."

Eel smiled. "I believe it."

When the alarm went off at three a.m. Callie flung her hand out from under the covers and pushed the button. She kept her eyes closed for a few minutes longer, then heaved a sigh and sat up in the darkness, listening to the radio softly playing in Viola's room. A crack of light seeped under the bedroom door and spilled all the way to the window. By the time she got up, dressed and went downstairs, Viola was already waiting for her.

"Is this Sunday?" Callie whispered.

"You know it is," replied Viola, opening the front door.

"I don't remember how we came to this arrangement. Remind me. Why is it that Cele gets to sleep in on Sundays and we don't?"

"Because she's bigger than us, remember? You really want to go through that argument again?"

"I suppose not."

They walked out to the car and got in, Viola at the wheel.

Callie stared out at the streetlights glistening on the wet pavement. Viola gave her a half smile. "She'll make it up to us someday. You know that."

"Yeah. Sure she will."

They rode in silence on the short drive to the bakery. Once inside, they got busy mixing up dough for the sweet rolls, cookies and breads, which would be warm and fragrant by seven a.m.

As the scent of cinnamon and coffee filled the room, Callie's tired muscles relaxed. No matter how weary she might be, or how discouraged, she loved the first hours of morning, when the day was new and unspoiled. Her sunny morning disposition set her apart from her sisters, and, in spite of her grumbling, she much preferred the morning shift to the afternoon. She loved being able to walk out at one o'clock with the rest of the day free.

She was almost done when the bell above the door rang. Haven stepped in, blocking the light.

He smiled confidently. "Hi. Thought I'd surprise you."

Callie wiped her hands on her apron and smiled back, caught off-guard by a momentary flight instinct. Ordinarily, she would be happy to spend her Sunday afternoon with her idealistic boyfriend. But today she had been looking forward to a quiet afternoon on the lake with Rugby. The sun was out for a change, and she longed to feel it on her skin. Seeing the enthusiasm in Haven's eyes, however, she pushed down her own desires.

"Well, you did," she said. "I thought you had to be in Olympia today."

"I don't have to be there till tomorrow morning. It's such a nice day, I thought we could have a picnic by the Locks."

She forced another smile and said, "Let me just tell Vi I'm leaving."

An hour later, seated on the grassy bank overlooking the Chittendon Locks, Callie closed her eyes and reveled in the sun on her face. Beside her, Haven was going on about his latest efforts to lobby for more stringent regulations on the growing number of cruise ships visiting Seattle. Callie had heard the argument so many times she could almost deliver it herself, but she knew better than to try to stop Haven. After two years of dating, she understood her role. Whenever Haven was preparing to go on one of his missions, he would go over his arguments with her. Repeatedly.

She opened her eyes and glanced at him. He stopped in mid-phrase and asked, "Don't you agree?"

"Of course," she responded without hesitation. She hadn't really been listening, but she knew her line. Haven wasn't like some philosophy or English majors, who raise questions for the fun of arguing about them. He had done the research and was firmly convinced that he was right. Discussion was not an option.

Eventually Haven reached a stopping point and looked out at the boats lined up to go through the locks. Callie wondered if he could appreciate the beauty of the scene without thinking about all the troubling environmental aspects of motor boats.

But his next comment surprised her.

"So. What have you been up to lately? I know you've been busy with your little show. I'm sorry I couldn't get there this weekend. I'll try to be there next weekend."

"Oh. It's okay. I know you have important things to do. It went well. People seemed to like it."

Haven nodded. "And how are your classes coming?" At twenty-four, Haven was through with higher education, but he was encouraging Callie to aim for a doctorate, to give her more credibility in the political arena. Not that Callie had any political aspirations, but Haven already had penciled her into his.

"They're fine. Everything's going okay, I guess." She pulled at a blade of grass, curling it round her finger as she spoke. She considered telling him about the baby otter, but the words stuck in her throat. This would be a perfect time to tell him about her exciting discovery and rescue. Still she hesitated. He'd probably pat her on the head and tell her she did a nice thing, and that would be that. She frowned and broke the blade of grass in two. There was no need to tell him about Puki.

Haven smiled at her, and she smiled back. The sun was beginning to sink lower behind the hills of Magnolia. Haven stretched and said,

"I guess we ought to be going. I'd ask you to come over, but I'll be leaving before six in the morning."

"That's okay. I have a lot of studying to do," she said, not meeting his eyes.

When he dropped her off at the house, they kissed, but he didn't get out of the car. She wrapped her sweater around her shoulders as she walked up to the door. Rugby was waiting inside and jumped on her legs when she came in. "Okay, okay. Just give me a second," she said. She grabbed the leash and a plastic bag before going out into the dusk.

CHAPTER SIX

In the misty light of Monday morning, Callie returned to her classes and tried to focus on the life cycle of coral, kelp-based ecosystems, and the changing habits of orca whales.

When she came out of her last class at four o'clock, she gave in to the impulse to visit Puki. The bus to downtown rumbled over the Montlake Cut, where a pair of kayaks were skimming toward the marshy preserve behind Husky stadium. The clouds above were pearly gray, with streaks of darkness that promised rain by nightfall.

At the aquarium she hurried up the wooden ramp, flashed her member's card, and went straight to the otters' pool. They were slipping and sliding through the water as usual, somersaulting and paddling on their backs as they groomed their faces. Puki was playing with one of the other young otters. Callie's heart lifted at the sight of him.

Out of the corner of her eye, she saw something shift in the darkness on the other side of the tank. She peered deeper into the glass and realized she was being watched. She drew back and looked away. When she risked another glance across the tank, the face had vanished.

She heard a rustle behind her and turned. He was so close she noticed a scent of wet leaves that seemed part of him.

"Hey," he said softly.

"Hello," she replied. He was awfully close.

"You were amazing the other night."

She frowned in confusion.

"Saturday. The LIP thing? You and your sisters. Fantastic."

Callie smiled slowly. "You were there?"

"Yeah. Friend of a friend dragged me. If I'd known you were in it, I wouldn't have resisted."

Callie tried to curb her smile. "Really?"

"You guys are good. I liked the songs. I'm not usually much for the folky type. But you got something special."

"Well, thanks. I'm glad you liked it."

"Do you play around?"

"What do you mean?"

"Clubs. Where d'you play?"

"Oh. No. We don't perform all that much. We do some festivals and street fairs."

"Huh. Have you got a CD?"

"Mmm, no. We haven't gotten around to it."

"You should. Stupid not to."

She stiffened slightly. "Yes. Well. We have other things to do."

Eel stared quietly at her until she bristled and said, "Would you stop that please?"

"What?"

"Staring."

"Can't help it."

"Yes, you can."

"What if I don't want to?"

She rolled her eyes. "Fine. Knock yourself out." She turned back toward the otters. "I only came to see how my baby's doing."

"He's great. I been keepin' an eye on him."

They watched the otters for a few minutes.

"I like the name," he said. "What's your name, anyway?"

She squared her shoulders. "My name is Callie. Short for Calliope."

Eel raised an eyebrow. She shrugged.

"And what do they call you?" she asked.

"Eel."

"That's not your real name."

"It's real enough. It's on my CD."

"You have a CD?"

"It's not that hard."

"I guess not." Callie had an idea she was grinning at him more than she should.

Eel was staring at her again, with a smile of his own, and she realized that she was staring back. "I could help you, if you like. With the CD," he said.

She shifted her weight. "Maybe. We'll see. I'll talk to my sisters." She looked away. "I better go."

"Can I call you?" he blurted. It was a phrase he had never used.

"That's probably not a good idea." She paused, as if considering saying something else, then said, "I'm sure I'll run into you here again." She was starting to turn away when a wet sponge ball flew out of the tank and splashed on her chest. She jumped back with a little shriek and stared into the tank where Puki was treading water and staring at her.

"Did you throw that?" she demanded, without considering whether asking an otter a question made sense. She glanced at Eel, who was watching Puki.

"I can't believe he did that," she said.

"Me neither. Do otters usually do that kind of thing?"

"What? Throw things at people? Like seals? I don't think so. I mean, they're playful, but I've never seen that happen before."

Eel knelt down to make better eye contact with Puki. "Hey buddy," he said, "You know it's not nice to splash people who aren't in the pool."

"I don't mind," Callie said. "Really. It was just... I wasn't expecting it. I wonder why he did it?"

Eel picked up the sponge ball and tossed it back to Puki. The otter grabbed it out of the air and dove underwater with it. Eel glanced at Callie. "You better be ready," he said.

"You don't think he'd—" The sopping wet ball flew at her again, but this time she managed to catch it before it soaked her shirt. She grinned at Puki and said, "You want to play catch, huh?"

Puki shook his head. Callie looked at Eel. "Did you see that?"

"I saw it. I just can't believe it. Has to be coincidence. He can't understand what we say. Can he?"

Callie's heart was racing, her nerves twitching. In spite of herself, she couldn't stop the thought from taking shape: What if Puki was sent to her for a reason? She tossed the sponge farther into the tank, out of his reach. He remained treading water in front of her and Eel, looking from one to the other. Then he tilted his head to one side and made a funny chirruping sound before diving under and swimming to the other end of the tank.

Callie waited for him to come back. When he didn't return, Eel stood up and looked at her with a question in his eyes. She hoped he wouldn't spoil it by saying something stupid. But he turned back toward the tank, and together they watched Puki resume his play with the older otters, until Callie felt too edgy to stay another minute.

"I have to go," she said.

Eel didn't ask why.

She studied his face. "You won't tell anyone what just happened, will you? I mean, I guess if he starts throwing the ball to other people—"

"That won't happen. He likes you. He likes me. Maybe there's a reason."

She stared into Eel's eyes, but she couldn't find a word to say.

So she turned and walked away.

He wanted to run after her, to convince her somehow that he wasn't the loser she seemed to think he was, but he was lost in a labyrinth of thought. He was used to feeling he was the center of his own world. But now, as if a new magnetic pole had formed, his gravitational field was realigned around a girl named Calliope, and he didn't believe it was a coincidence.

As she hurried away down the sidewalk, the Calliope girl was herself a bit mystified. Her skin tingled as if she had dived into an icy pool. The sensation was at once shocking and intoxicating. She walked fast, trying to stay ahead of the dizzying emotions bubbling up in her wake. What was it about that guy? He was a nothing. A nobody. A slacker with no moral center. Probably. Callie slowed her pace. He had some kind of connection with Puki. She'd seen it. He wasn't making it up. She frowned at the fading light in the sky and tried to understand why she felt this need to keep her distance. Being close to him made her feel jumpy. Or was it something else?

She dug her hands into her jacket pockets. Feeling the first drops of rain, she turned her face upward and closed her eyes, savoring the blessing, the silver curtain that kept the tourists away for nine months of every year.

With its tiara of snow-rimmed peaks visible at the end of every avenue, its necklace of lakes and waterways that sparkled around every bend, and the giant evergreens that loomed like Ents with their heads in the clouds, Seattle sometimes seemed a kind of fantasy realm, where Hobbits and Faire Folk might easily find lodgings. Since earliest childhood, when her grandfather would take her down to the shipyard in Ballard, where gulls screamed all day and big ships moved with the implacable bulk of icebergs, Callie had felt a kinship with the city that went beyond words. Her sisters mocked her rapturous responses to the natural beauty they took for granted. Only her grandfather encouraged the little girl, and promised that her "gift for the sea" was a treasure to be cherished.

The bus arrived, and Callie got on. She stared out at the dark streets through the rain-streaked window and thought, not for the first time, that living here felt the way she imagined it would be inside a bubble at the bottom of the sea. It only lacked a few sharks swimming by the window.

She shivered slightly, as her thoughts swam into a memory of Eel. His intensity unsettled her. She didn't care to analyze the feeling, but she couldn't deny that she was intrigued by him, and she wouldn't mind seeing more of him. In the fantastic realm of her own private Seattle, Eel looked right at home.

Yet that didn't explain the Puki connection. And there was no way she was going to get into it with Eel. How could he possibly understand? He probably just thought all otters were cute and playful. Which they are. But she couldn't shake the idea that Puki was something more.

All her life Callie had tried to rein in her fanciful imagination, determined not to follow the crazy path her mother had chosen. But what if Puki was a messenger? What if her mother had something to do with it? What if after all these years, there was something real to make sense of all the pain?

The next morning Eel woke much too early for a day off. He had stayed up late playing his guitar and smoking cigarettes, thinking about Callie and trying to come up with a plan for seeing her again. Eventually he had realized that he was never going to get anywhere if he only saw her while he was at work. It was too easy for her to walk away. Around midnight a brilliant idea occurred to him. He would find out where she worked and confront her there. She'd have to talk to him.

The girl at the LIP Festival had mentioned a bakery, but he didn't remember a name. He would simply have to visit each one until he found her.

Celeste was cleaning a table by the front window when she noticed a guy with a green Mohawk staring at the bakery from across the street. Noting his black leather jacket, sunglasses, and tight, ragged jeans, she said, "Oh look! We have a new contender in the Poser of the Month contest."

At the word 'poser' Callie's ears pricked up. She set down the bowl of icing she'd been stirring and edged toward the front of the bakery. Catching sight of the fan of green hair, she was tip-toeing closer when Viola came up behind her. "Avoiding someone?"

Callie jumped with a little squeak of surprise. Celeste turned at the sound and asked gleefully, "You know him? Oh my God—has our golden girl been dabbling in the Dark Side?"

Callie frowned and blushed at the same time. "I do not know him. He's just someone I pulled out of the lake."

Celeste grinned. "Nice catch."

"What was I supposed to do? Let him drown?"

Viola, with her arms crossed in front of her chest, stared out the window. "Guys like that don't go boating. Are you sure it was him?"

"It was him. I'd know that smirk anywhere."

"Oh really?" said Celeste, raising her eyebrows at Viola. "Correct me if I'm wrong, and I'm sure you will, but I'm sensing a frisson of chemistry here. Did sparks fly between you guys out there on the lake?"

Callie snorted. "Sparks don't fly when one of you is soaking wet. Although he did try to light a cigarette. That's when I told him to jump back in the lake."

Celeste and Viola exchanged a glance.

Viola ran a hand through her spiky hair as she continued to study Eel. "He's kind of cute in a little-boy-lost-in-black-leather, please-someone-notice-me kind of way."

Callie pursed her lips and assumed a busy attitude, rearranging the pastries in the case.

"I wonder if he'd like a muffin," mused Viola.

Celeste laughed. "Oh come on, Vi. He doesn't look like the muffin type."

"A cruller, you think?"

Celeste laughed louder. "Oh no. Definitely nothing from the doughnut family. He's clearly a rebel. Maybe a scone."

"A rolling scone."

As her sisters' laughter grew louder and their suggestions sillier, Callie kept her head down, hoping Eel's presence across the street was a coincidence. But when the tinkle of the front door bell interrupted her sisters, Callie straightened up behind the counter, and there he was.

She felt her cheeks turning pink and cursed her fair skin for its lack of cool. Eel smiled.

"So this is where you work." He nodded. "'S nice."

Callie eyed him skeptically. "Do you want something?"

He gave her a look, then peered in the cases brimming with sugary pastries and buttery rolls. "Are those any good?" he asked, pointing to some cherry Danish.

"Everything's good," she replied curtly.

He gave her another look. "I'll have one of those then."

"For here or to go?"

Eel eyed the three small tables by the window. "For here." He watched her put the Danish on a plate. As she handed it to him, he said, "I hate to eat alone. Can you sit with me for a minute?"

Callie frowned. She said in a gentler tone, "I'm sorry. I can't sit down while I'm working. My sisters would get mad."

"No we wouldn't," Celeste piped up from behind her. "Would we, Vi?"

"Not at all. Go ahead, Callie. You deserve a break, what with all that heavy lifting you do."

This remark set off another gale of laughter, and Callie rolled her eyes and said, "Okay, fine. But you guys go on in the back."

"Right." Celeste smiled at Eel. "Nice not meeting you."

"Likewise," said Viola as they backed away into the kitchen.

Eel gave Callie a questioning look, but she just shook her head and said, "Do you have sisters?"

"Nope."

"Figures."

"What do you mean by that?" He remained standing at the counter, holding the plate in front of him.

"Nothing. It's just another thing we don't have in common. That brings it up to about a thousand."

"You've been counting?"

A titter sounded from the kitchen. Callie sighed and said, "Just sit down, okay?"

Eel took a seat and waited, but before she came from behind the counter the bell over the door jingled again. A tall, broad-shouldered, blonde guy, with the muscled look and ruddy complexion of a serious outdoorsman, walked in. Eel took an instant dislike to him, which intensified when the guy addressed Callie as "sweetie."

Eel caught the embarrassed glance Callie stole at him, and took some comfort from it. But when the guy leaned over the counter and kissed her on the lips, and Callie didn't slap him, Eel's gut churned. He listened shamelessly while the guy talked to her.

Since the guy had his back to him and was speaking rapidly, Eel couldn't get all of it, but it sounded like he was trying to convince Callie to do something. After some discussion, the guy's voice took on an authoritative tone, as he said, "You know I'm right, Callie. You want to do this. I'm asking you to do this. There's nothing more to discuss. I'll call you tonight." With that, he turned and left.

Eel made no attempt to disguise that he'd been listening. He stared at Callie and said, "If there's nothing more to discuss, I don't see why he has to call you tonight."

Callie burst into laughter. She laughed until tears started at the corners of her eyes, and then she wiped them away with her apron and tried to control the smile that showed in her eyes. "He's not always..." she began, and then stopped. She let out a breath and looked down at the floor.

Eel came over to the counter. "He your boyfriend?"

"He's not my boyfriend."

Eel raised his eyebrows. "Does he know that?"

Callie laughed again, but finished with a sigh. "It's complicated."

Eel caught her eye and said in a quiet tone that sent shivers down her neck, "Listen, maybe we don't have anything in common, but I'd like to change that. Could you meet me after work sometime? Maybe get coffee. Or fish. Or dog food."

"Dog food?"

"Not for us. For your dog. You know. I'm flexible."

Callie shook her head, but she kept smiling. "Let's start with coffee."

"Right. Save the dog food for our second date."

"It's not a date."

"Didn't say it was."

Callie stared into his eyes and tried to find the anger she usually felt toward guys who pestered her, but something about Eel doused her wrath and left her feeling thirsty instead.

"I get off in an hour."

"I'll be back." He strolled out the door.

Through the window, Callie watched him walk away, and noticed idly that the sun was poking through the clouds. A precious sun break. The light caught Eel's green hair, and for a moment Callie felt the world around her shift. Then he disappeared, the sun break ended, and she went back to the ovens.

By the time she got off work, she wished hadn't agreed to have coffee. In spite of her protest, she knew that Haven considered himself her boyfriend, and up until a few months ago, she had felt sure of her feelings for him. But lately she was beginning to have doubts about the whole tangled mess of idealism and commitment.

"You feeling all right?"

Callie started. She hadn't noticed his approach. "Yeah. I'm just a little beat."

"Long day?"

"Oh, I was lucky today. I didn't have to do the early shift. I got here at six-thirty."

"You're kidding. When does the early shift start?"

"We start mixing the first dough at three-thirty."

"In the morning?"

"Yup."

"Well, let's get you some coffee then."

As they walked, Eel asked questions about the bakery, and Callie answered, aware that she was avoiding the brush-off she should be delivering. She didn't want to lead him on. So why wasn't she telling him goodbye?

The fragrance of fresh-roasted coffee filled the air at the Bean Scene. They sat in a booth by the window. Callie looked Eel in the eye and said, "Listen—"

Eel held up his hand. "I know," he interrupted, "you like me as a friend, but that's all, because Studly Do-right is the Chosen One?"

The gentleness in his voice left Callie feeling more uncomfortable than she'd expected. If only he'd been nasty, it would have been easy to blow him off.

"Well, something like that. I wasn't being totally honest when I said Haven wasn't my boyfriend."

Eel lifted his eyebrows a fraction.

"We've been together for two years, but a lot of it is because we share the same ideals. He's very dedicated to the environment. He's done a lot of important work."

"Well that's great. I'm all for the environment. And as long as he makes you happy..." Eel kept his gaze leveled on her. Callie shifted uneasily and drank some of her coffee, which was still too hot.

The cafe's sound system was playing a quirky trio of accordion, clarinet and guitar, a hybrid Cajun-gypsy dance tune, and Callie couldn't stop her knee from bouncing in time. Suddenly her knee came up against Eel's, and he smiled so happily that, without intending to, Callie smiled brightly back.

"Good band," he said.

"Yeah."

"Maybe you and me could make music together sometime."

Callie pushed her cup away. "I don't think that would be a good idea."

"Why not? You don't even know what I play."

"I can guess."

"Oh really?" Eel leaned back in his chair, his expression blank.

Callie detected warning signs in his face, but she ignored them. "I'm guessing you don't play folk music. Or love songs. Maybe some old-school rock and roll. But more thrash and slash. Rage against the empire stuff." She folded her arms and said, "Am I wrong?"

Eel's face was a mask of indifference. He reached inside his jacket for a pack of cigarettes, drew one out and returned the pack to its pocket before he spoke. "Wrong? How could you be wrong?"

He tapped the cigarette on the table and pulled out a lighter.

"You aren't planning to light that in here are you?" she asked.

"Right again," he said, his mouth hardening into a frown. He returned the lighter to his pocket and the cigarette to the pack, and they sat without speaking until they both began at once.

"You know smoking really is bad for you—"

"Why do you stay with him?"

"It's not something I want to talk about with you."

"Right. Cause it'll go away if you don't talk about it." He stared intently at her. "Or wait, no it won't. It's your life that will go down the drain, while you let Daddy-Knows-Best tell you what to do."

She glowered at him. "Listen, you don't know anything about Haven. He's a very courageous and smart person who's trying to do something meaningful with his life." She paused, feeling on the brink of going too far, but unable to stop herself. "Unlike some people."

Eel nodded. He looked into her eyes with an expression she couldn't parse. He shrugged and said, "Well. I guess that's it then, innit? Mr. Savin' the World, eh?" He stood up and bowed slightly to her. "Guess you were right after all. We'll never have anything in common."

And with that, he turned and left without a backward glance.

Moments later, behind the wheel, Eel smoked with a furious intensity. She thought she had him all figured out. The bitch. Why was he wasting his time with her anyway? There were plenty of girls who wouldn't hassle him every time he lit a smoke. Hell, they bought him smokes. He jammed the butt into the ashtray and glared at an old woman hobbling across the street in front of him. "You wouldn't last a minute in D.C.," he muttered.

It had been quite an adjustment—the whole 'brake for pedestrians' thing that was treated like a cardinal rule in the Pacific Northwest. And jaywalking? Forget it. At first Eel had found it amusing, waiting in the rain at deserted street corners for the light to change. But right now his temper was frayed, as if he'd been slapped in the face. Who did she think she was? Judging him like she was some kind of... He let his foot slide off the accelerator. A vision of her face rose in his mind as he remembered the sound of her singing. Eventually he shook himself and stepped on the gas.

He got to the aquarium just before the regular closing time. Susan Anderson, the activities coordinator, was standing in the lobby with a harried look, balancing a box of flyers and an armful of flowers. She beamed at him when he walked in.

"Oh Eel, you're here. Thank goodness. I was afraid you might have forgotten."

"Yeah. I get that a lot," Eel said.

"Oh, no. I don't mean that I think you aren't reliable, it's just, you've never done one of these after-hours events and I—"

"'S all right. No worries. What do you want me to do?"

Ms. Anderson quickly went over the schedule for the evening. One of the downtown law firms had rented the aquarium for the night to host a celebration for a new partner.

The lobby soon filled with a crowd of youngish-looking professional types. Eel lurked in the shadows, making sure no one strayed into the off-limits sections. Late in the evening he shooed one couple out of the otter area when he heard the man joking about pouring his drink into the water. "I was just kidding," the man protested.

Left alone with the otters, Eel peered into the tank, looking for Puki. The little otter slithered up close to the glass and did a flip right in front of Eel, then bobbed to the surface, looked up at him, and winked.

Eel stared. The otter quickly did another somersault, and popped up and winked again. The room spun around Eel as if he'd just stepped off a moving carousel.

"You winkin' at me buddy?" he whispered.

Puki swam back and forth rapidly, chirping in his odd little way. Then he rolled onto his back and waved one of his flipper paws at Eel.

Eel grinned. "You are, aren't you?"

Puki nodded his head two or three times. Then he flipped back on his stomach and dove out of sight.

Eel stood in the darkness waiting for his return, but the little otter swam to the other side of the pool and began nuzzling one of the older otters. Eel stood still, unwilling to break the magic of the moment, until he heard someone calling him from the party room. Reluctantly he walked away.

Later, after the crowd had gone and he was cleaning up, Eel went back to the otter tank several times to see if Puki would repeat his performance. But the baby otter appeared oblivious, playing nonstop with his tank mates. Eel almost wondered if he'd imagined the whole thing, but the memory was too vivid. It was real. The baby otter knew him. And, what was more, Puki liked him. Eel was sure of it. He couldn't help reflecting on the way Callie had dismissed him. *So you lose the girl but get the otter. Could be worse.*

It was after two in the morning by the time Eel drove home. He was waiting at a stoplight in the U District when he saw a group of five kids at the corner. It was unclear whether they were waiting for a bus, or the light to change, or for their lives to begin.

They were all wearing tight, ragged jeans and black jackets or hooded sweatshirts, and several of them had some manner of facial hair. One had the exaggerated mutton chop sideburns embraced by devotees of the pirate motif. Another had the beginnings of a goatee. They were all pierced in some way—nose, cheek, eyebrows. Tattoos crept like black growths on their necks.

Eel almost nodded at them in solidarity. They so plainly fit the profile of wannabe punk bands from New York to LA. But his sense of camaraderie turned sour as his eye lingered on one member of the group, a bit taller than the rest, whose hair was gelled into green spikes. Eel stared at the kid, taking in his black leather jacket, his motorcycle boots, the cigarette dangling from his lip, the sullen pout on his pale face.

The car behind him honked, and Eel frowned, noticing the light had changed. He stepped on the gas, but as he pulled away, he took one last look in his side mirror at the cluster of punks huddled in the cold beam of the street light.

CHAPTER SEVEN

Callie reached inside her windbreaker and tried to find a dry tissue without dropping the pile of flyers or her umbrella. The rain was coming sideways, driven by a cold wind off the Sound.

The wind helped carry Haven's voice into the crowd gathered at Pier 66. Many of the protesters brandished signs with the slogan, "You cruise, we lose!" Callie stood at the edge of the group, handing out flyers to passersby. Most refused the flyers. Some took them and threw them in the trash. Only a few stopped to listen to Haven.

Behind him, a giant cruise ship loomed like a modern day Trojan horse, and Callie braced for the conflict that was coming. Haven planned to block tourists from leaving the boat, to call attention to the destruction of the marine ecosystem. The ship owners wouldn't be the only ones to resent Haven's plan. Local merchants relied upon tourists for income, and tourists paid good money to visit Seattle by boat. Haven said they had to draw a line to make city officials recognize the gravity of the problem and the real threat to the sea life on which the region's local economy depended.

Callie shivered and wiped her nose again. It was almost May, but the air still had the raw bite of mid-March. She shuffled her feet on the wet sidewalk and peered back at the cruise ship, where the first batch of sightseers was starting down the ramp to the pier. Haven's crowd surged forward, closing the gap. A group of protesters linked arms, with Haven at the center, and formed a wall blocking the exit at the bottom of the ramp. When the tourists reached the blockade, they demanded to be allowed to pass. Haven's refusal was louder. He began describing the negative impact of the large ships on the marine habitat. Callie couldn't hear exactly what he was saying, but the mood of the tourists was unmistakable. Cries of "Shut up!" and "Get out of the way!" rose above the general noise.

A marching-band drumbeat accompanied Haven's supporters as they chanted "Seattle refuses oversized cruises!" Callie strained to see Haven, but the crowd was swelling rapidly with more tourists wandering over from the neighboring area to see the commotion. Police cars arrived with their blue lights flashing, and wailing sirens added to the din.

Suddenly there was a loud bang and the protesters retreated like a tide of denim. As Callie pushed forward to see, someone's elbow slammed into her face. She yelled and pushed back, and when she got clear of the mob, she saw Haven with his back to the cruise ship, his jaw jutting toward two cops, one of the whom had a gun pointed at Haven.

Callie tried to get closer, but she was unable to force her way through the crowd. She could hear the cops talking and the crowd jeering. One of the cops turned to them and said, "Anyone else here want to get arrested?"

A half dozen students stepped forward, but the rest edged away, muttering, their protest signs drooping in the falling rain. While the cops clamped handcuffs on Haven and a couple of protesters, the tourists slipped down the ramp and scurried off toward the Pike Place shops.

Callie gathered up her wet flyers and trudged to the bus stop. Obviously Haven wouldn't be giving her a ride home. She considered stopping in at The Sounding to check on Puki, but balked at the thought that she might run into Eel. She didn't feel up to another sparring match. She'd had enough conflict for one day.

The next morning the sun returned, lighting up the east slope of Mount Rainier and causing delays on the floating bridges as motorists slowed to steal a peek at the elusive mountain's majesty.

Sunlight shafted through Eel's room, gifting the dusty air with a moment of glamour, while he lay in bed staring at the cracked plaster in the ceiling, measuring his body's call for nicotine, and wondering why. What was stopping him from lighting up a cigarette? First smoke of the day. Arguably the best. Eel reached for the pack muttering, "Why shouldn't I?"

But as his fingers found the matches and flipped them open with a practiced, one-handed move, he paused, and in that pause he held his breath and clenched his jaw. Silence surrounded him, offering no help. He sat up and a sliver of sunlight cut across his cheek. He stared at the cigarette.

He returned it to the pack and tossed the pack across the room. He stood up and went to the mirror and examined the straggling green hair that fell to his shoulders. He grabbed it in a ponytail and pulled it back, turning his head from side to side. Then he reached for a shirt from his backpack. The sparsely furnished room held no chest of drawers. Eel's few clothes were still bundled in the backpack he'd carried along with his guitar all the way from Virginia. He pawed through the selection and finally chose a black t-shirt. He pulled it over his head, slid into his jeans, and went to find some scissors.

Later that day when Eel returned to the aquarium, Susan stopped him in the hall and asked if he had enjoyed working the late shift. When he said he didn't mind it, her face brightened, and she quickly explained how the night watchman had quit unexpectedly, and would Eel be interested in filling the vacancy?

"I understand you have a musical career, but if you think you could help us out, even for a short time while we look for someone permanent, that would be wonderful," she said.

Eel ran a hand through his shorn hair. He had no bookings in the foreseeable future. Mitch had stopped looking for gigs since he had moved in with Natalie, and, in his new state of mind, Eel wasn't sure he would take a gig if one came along. His nights were wide open. Plus, there was the baby otter. And the thought of Puki led to thoughts of Callie. Eel wasn't sure how she would feel about him bonding with the baby otter, but it was too late. He was already connected. He nodded to Susan and said, "Yeah. I can do that."

She smiled gratefully. "That's wonderful! Let me show you the log and get you some keys, and we can go over the routine."

A half hour later Eel was back out on Alaska Way. Now that he didn't have to be at work till evening, he had time to kill. He resisted the urge to go by the bakery and tell Callie about his new position at the aquarium. She'd made it clear she couldn't care less. So he went home and spent the rest of the day alternately playing guitar and trying to sleep, since he would be up all night.

Upon returning from class the next day, Callie burst into the living room, and headed straight to the answering machine. Seeing there were no messages, she went into the kitchen and found Viola staring out the window.

"Did Haven call?" Callie asked.

"I thought he was in jail."

"He is. But usually he calls me to come get him, after they post his bail."

Viola shrugged. "Maybe they haven't set bail yet."

Callie frowned. "It's not like him not to call. I hope he's all right." She noticed that Viola was still staring out the window and asked, "What are you looking at?"

"A tree guy."

"You hired someone?"

"Our sister did."

"Oh." Callie smirked. Celeste auditioned men as if she were casting for a leading man in a romantic comedy, and if she'd hired a tree man, odds were that he was a hottie. "Are you expecting him to fall?"

"For Celeste? Or out of the tree?"

"Both."

"Well, so far he seems to know what he's doing up there. We'll have to wait and see how he does on the ground." Viola took a seat at the kitchen table. "So, your boyfriend's in jail. That's good, right? Isn't that what he wanted?"

"Yeah. I just worry about him."

Celeste came in from the living room. "Who? Haven? That guy's always all right. Who could bother him? I'm sure he can take care of himself."

"I know. It's just... usually he calls."

"He hasn't called?"

"No."

"Maybe he had to use his call for something else. Like a lawyer." Celeste went to the window and peered out. "Wow," she said. "I love a guy who understands rope."

"And you call me a freak," said Callie.

"Hey. I call 'em like I see 'em. And that guy," she nodded toward the window, "he could be a keeper."

"That's what you always say. Talk to me in a week."

"Don't be so quick to judge. Wait till you see him. Like a cross between Tarzan and Bob Dylan."

Callie shook her head. "I can't picture that."

Celeste grinned. "Oh come on, you're not trying. Just think scrawny but strong, wild hair, great abs and soulful eyes. It's a killer combination."

"Where did you find him?"

"That's the beauty part. He comes highly recommended by our own dear sister's earthy man."

"Henry knows him?"

"Yeah. Apparently Finn does a lot of work for the local beekeepers. Henry heard about him and hired him to shape up a pear tree, and I happened to be dropping Vi off, and one thing led to another."

"It always does with you."

"You're just jealous."

"Think what you like."

"I think when you see my Green Man you're going to want one for yourself."

"Your what?" Callie asked. For some reason the term resonated, like a coin tossed into a well. The distant sound of the splash sent a shiver down her neck.

"Green Man. That's the name of his tree business. It's a Celtic thing."

Callie looked out at the tall chestnut which shaded most of the tiny yard. "What did you tell him to do anyway? I love that tree."

"I do too. Don't worry, he's just giving it a little trim, like a haircut, cutting off the split ends, letting in some light."

"And when he's done?"

"Oh, a Green Man's work is never done," said Celeste.

Callie turned away from the window. "Maybe I should go down there."

"Down where?" asked Viola. "The jail?"

"Yeah. At least I could talk to Haven and find out what's going on."

"What makes you think they'd let you talk to him?"

"Oh come on. Why wouldn't they let me talk to him?"

Viola shrugged. "I'm just saying. If he's still in jail, maybe he wants to be. He might get more publicity staying in jail."

When she got to the jail, Callie learned that Haven was still locked up, though bail had been set at a mere two thousand dollars.

"Hey," she said, sitting down across from him in the visiting room. "Why are you still here? I thought you were going to call me."

He barely smiled at her. "It's all right, Callie. You shouldn't worry. I would have called you, but it's important that we make the most of this situation, so I called the newspaper."

Callie took a closer look at him. He seemed calm, but his eyes shone with excitement.

"Luckily, the reporter I spoke with got it right away. She came down last night and interviewed me. She seemed exceptionally intelligent for a news person. She told me they'd probably run the story in today's paper, unless they decide to make it a bigger story and go after the cruise ship operators."

Callie nodded. "So... you met with a reporter. But you didn't try to call me?"

Haven frowned slightly. "Callie? I knew you would understand. I thought you would understand. Don't you see? If we can get the papers to really give us some coverage, we can get people talking about the issue. And if we get people talking, the politicians will take notice. We have to get the story out. Thank God they arrested me! Now we've got some traction."

"Traction?"

"That's what Sandra calls it."

"Who's Sandra?"

"The reporter. Sandra Hulling. She's young, but she seems bright, and she's on our side."

"Huh." Callie leaned back in her chair. "So... how long are you planning to stay in jail?"

"I don't know. Our lawyer is coming later to discuss strategy. What we want is to appear in court and bring the truth about the damage to the marine ecosystem to the front page."

"That sounds great," said Callie, shrinking back in her seat.

Haven looked over her head to the door behind her. "That might be him now." He stood up. "You don't mind, do you, Callie? I've got things to do."

She got up quickly. "No, of course not. I'm glad things are going well. Let me know if you need me for anything."

Looking past her, Haven said, "Thanks, Cal."

"Bye," she said, and turned to go, nearly running into a man in a dark suit on his way in.

"Excuse me," he said.

She smiled tightly. When she glanced back, she saw Haven focused on the lawyer and talking fast.

She was in no mood to go home and face her sisters' questions. She stumped along the sidewalk irritably. Of course she was proud of Haven for his principles, and his determination, and his courage. But, she mumbled, did it make her a bad person to wish every once in a while he would show some sign of being crazy about her? Was that asking too much?

A dog barked at her. She looked up and realized she'd already marched halfway up First Hill, several blocks farther than she'd intended. She turned around and started retracing her footsteps, squinting into the sun that had abruptly come out.

Above the rooftops she saw the light gilding the Sound and felt an irresistible urge to get closer to it. Without thinking she broke into a jog and headed west.

Ten minutes later she stood in front of the aquarium, flushed and sweaty, wondering why she had come. She didn't want to admit to herself that the thought of Eel was somehow mixed up with her desire to check on Puki. There was no denying the flutter in her chest.

She flashed her pass at the entrance and went down the shadowy walkway to the otter tanks. Her heart lifted as she spied Puki skimming along the water, and she watched him cavort with his playmates for a while. Eventually she looked around, but there was no sign of Eel. In the past, it had seemed that all she had to do was enter the building, and he would materialize as if he had some kind of personal radar locked on her signal.

Today only tourists and volunteers ambled past the otter tank. Callie asked one of the volunteers if the guy with the green hair was working today. He looked at her blankly and shook his head. "Haven't seen anybody like that."

Callie went to find one of the regular staff. She learned from the girl who managed ticket sales that Eel hadn't been around for days.

She scowled and left, thinking darkly, *I knew he wouldn't last. He probably never cared about Puki at all.*

By the time she reached the bus stop, Callie had worked herself into a snit about men in general. *All they ever do is hit on you, use you, lie to you and ignore you. Who needs that?*

On the bus home, a mild-mannered UW student asked if the seat next to her was taken. Callie snapped, "Does it look taken? Go for it. What do I care?" After the boy moved on and took another seat, she huffed quietly. *Is it my fault you have no self-esteem? I don't have to make you feel good about yourself just because you have puppy-dog eyes.* She glared out at the street all the way home, and when she got there she was in no mood to respond to her sisters' questions about Haven. They could read about him in the paper.

The following morning, Haven's name appeared prominently in a story about the cruise ship debate, along with a picture of him being led off in handcuffs at the protest.

"Gee. Looks like your boyfriend's hit the big time," observed Celeste, folding the paper in half on the breakfast table.

Callie took a sip from her tea.

"He must be pretty pleased about the attention," continued Celeste.

"All men like attention," muttered Callie.

Celeste looked over the paper at her. "Do I detect a critical note? Doesn't everyone like attention, regardless of gender?"

"I've got work to do," Callie said, and went upstairs to her room. The truth was, she didn't have any pressing work, but she didn't feel like discussing her boyfriend at the moment. Stray bullets of anger kept shooting through her mind. She didn't know why she was so irritated with Haven. He hadn't done anything wrong. He'd done exactly what he'd said he was going to do, just as he always did. He was nothing if not reliable.

Out the window she watched the drizzle speckling the sidewalk and tried to breathe life into her feelings for Haven. Yet, though the check list of his admirable qualities was as long as ever, Callie didn't feel eager to see him. She could wait. If he wanted to stay in jail for a few weeks, even. Maybe absence would make her heart grow fonder. But, she wondered, as she watched circular ripples expand until they broke and vanished in the puddle by the curb, what if her feelings simply disappeared?

A pang of sadness hit her, yet she realized that it wasn't caused by the idea of losing Haven, but at the loss of her own conviction that her life had a higher purpose, a larger cause than her own happiness. She felt adrift and alone, and wished she had a mother she could turn to for comfort. She quickly shook off that desire, as she had schooled herself to do. Her mother had never been all that comforting. Radiant, wild, and exciting to be around, yes. But comforting? Not so much.

Callie was five years old when her mother left, saying she could no longer remain tied to a man who was content to bake bread for a living. Callie's father had tried to carry on and raise the three girls on his own, hoping she'd return. After a year with no word, he lost heart. He hung up his apron, handed the girls over to his parents, and went off in search of her.

That was the last anyone had seen of either of them. The grandparents had taken on the girls and raised them with love and care, Grandma Linden making sure they knew how to bake and sew and sing, Grandpa teaching them to fish and to sail a boat. It was soon apparent that Callie took to the water. She could manage a rowboat when she was five, and by the time she was seven, she could sail a small skiff single-handed. She wasn't afraid to bait a hook and could sit silent in a boat for hours, alone or with her grandfather. It was understood that of the three sisters, Callie was the water girl.

Callie had never told anyone, not even her grandfather, the secret her mother had told her, scarcely a week before she left.

The family had gone to Golden Gardens for a picnic. Her father was helping her sisters fly kites down on the beach, while her mother sat with Callie under the pines bordering the sand. She began talking quietly to Callie, and in urgent whispered words told the little girl a fairytale of wonder. She spoke of a life under the sea, of coral castles and sea turtle playmates. Callie didn't know what to make of it. She was not a silly girl. She'd seen pictures of Disney's Little Mermaid, and she knew that make-believe had nothing to do with real fish.

"So you see, Callie, that's why I have to go," her mother had said, pushing a strand of blonde hair off her face and staring out at the Sound. "A mermaid can only stay on land for seven years, and my time is up. I wanted you to know, because you're the one who carries the gift. You have it, Callie. You have the gift of the sea inside you."

She paused and looked down the beach to where Callie's father was laughing with her sisters.

Watching her, Callie frowned and asked, "Does Daddy know?"

Her mother turned to her with a half-smile. "He doesn't understand. He's only human."

Callie's frown deepened. "Aren't you?"

Her mother gazed out at the water, looking north where the Sound led to the ocean. "I am now, but soon I must return to the sea. It's where I belong. And so do you."

"How do you know?'

"Ask yourself, Callie. Where do you feel more at home? On the water? Or on the land?"

Callie said nothing, but stared out at the water. Her mother put an arm around her and pulled her closer.

"It's okay, Callie. You'll see. Because of your father, you aren't like me. You can stay on the land as long as you like, but you'll always have a special connection to the sea. When I'm gone, if you ever need help, you'll find it in the sea."

"How?"

"I can't tell you how. But that's where you'll find it. That I promise you."

At the sound of Celeste's happy chatter, they both turned to see her father coming. Her mother leaned close to Callie and whispered, "You must never tell anyone what I've told you. Promise me."

Callie nodded solemnly.

A few days later, when her father's anguished scream rent the air after he found her mother's cryptic note, Callie sat very still and didn't cry with her sisters. She hugged her knees to her chest and stared out at the rain, looking for patterns in the dark clouds.

Now, fifteen years later, Callie felt cut adrift from the purposeful future she had planned to share with Haven, or someone like him. As this realization grew, she felt a surge of guilt at her pragmatic estimation of Haven. He was a worthy, admirable man, but not irreplaceable in her heart. Suddenly she wondered if she was destined, like her mother, to seek some doomed dream.

She closed her eyes to block this vision of reckless romance. It wasn't what she wanted. But even with her eyes closed, she could see Eel, and the memory of his gaze enticed her beyond reason's puny reach.

CHAPTER EIGHT

Eel was playing his guitar quietly, unplugged, chasing a melody that had been whispering in his brain, when an unfamiliar buzzing interrupted his flow. For a moment he couldn't figure out where it was coming from. No one ever rang the buzzer. Few people ever visited.

He set down the guitar and shambled to the door, anticipating some kid with a sales pitch. He stared for a few seconds before he recognized two of the three people standing in the hall.

"What are you doing here?" he said, a grin slowly spreading on his face at the sight of Tommy Owens flanked by his girlfriend Abby and a short guy. The dimple in Tommy's cheek winked as he returned the smile and said, "Whoa! Nice to see you too. You mowed your hair."

Eel ran a hand over the ragged remains of his hair and shrugged. "Got tired of messing with it. Come on in."

"This is Squid," said Tommy, pointing a thumb at the shorter guy. "He's a musician too, from Berkeley."

"What do you play?" Eel asked.

"Keyboards mostly. Some bass."

"Squid sings too. He's got a really great voice," Abby added, her words accompanied by the tinkling of the silver hoops in her ears and the bangles on her wrists. A purple bandana held back the chestnut hair that fell below her shoulders.

Eel smiled at her. "I'll take your word for it."

They sat on the assortment of boxes and folding chairs that served as furniture, and Tommy did most of the talking.

"When Fergus told us you'd gone to Seattle, we decided to visit and hear the band," Tommy concluded.

Watching Abby, whose gray eyes lit up whenever Tommy spoke, Eel said, "Fergus should come here. Bring the family. The trees they got around here... he should see 'em."

"Yeah. He's still into trees. Not the way he was, you know, into that one." Tommy paused. "Sometimes I think about that tree—the one my dad cut down."

"The magic one?" asked Eel.

"Right. It was so small, you know? Compared to the ones up here." Tommy shrugged. "I guess it all worked out for the best."

Abby leaned closer to him and said, "Your mom and Fergus are happy. And we're happy. That's what matters."

Tommy gave a half-smile and said, "I guess so. How 'bout you, Eel? Is your band playing a lot?"

Eel shifted in his chair. "No band now."

"What? What happened? What about your CD?"

"There's lots of bands up here. Everybody's got a CD." He looked out the window. "I don't know. I'm workin' on some new things."

"So... you're still playing music?" While he questioned Eel, Tommy glanced uncertainly at Squid.

"Yeah. Still playing. Not sure why."

Squid nodded. Eel studied him, noticing the quiet style of dress— faded black jeans, faded gray sweatshirt, scuffed Chucks. Dark eyes stared out from a pale face framed by messy black hair.

"You in a band?" asked Eel.

"Been in bands. Not now."

"Still playing?"

"Yeah. Not sure why."

"I don't have a keyboard here."

"Mine's in the car. Be right back." Squid vanished out the door.

"Where'd you find him?" Eel asked.

"We went to hear a band in San Francisco one night, and he was in it. I thought of you when I heard him play. We talked to him afterward, and it turned out he was quitting that band because the rest of them wanted to move to LA, and Squid wasn't into that. We told him about you, and he said he'd always wanted to check out Seattle. So here we are."

Eel nodded. "'S not LA."

"Yeah. We noticed that already. Does the sun ever shine here?" Abby asked.

"People say it does. Haven't seen it myself. Might be one of those urban myths."

Squid reappeared with the keyboard. After he'd set up he looked at Eel expectantly.

Eel switched on his electric guitar and began playing a pattern of notes with a steady pulsing rhythm like oars dipping swiftly into water, pulling the melody forward. Squid joined in, adding a rich lower layer and swirling flourishes round the turns. Tommy and Abby bobbed their heads in time as the song grew bright and filled the room with energy.

They played for a good twenty minutes. Then they both stopped perfectly in sync. The air hummed for a few seconds, before Tommy said quietly, "Wow."

Sunlight darted past the shade and flickered across the bare wood floor. Eel and Squid looked at each other. Squid said, "When shall we three meet again?"

"Three?" said Eel.

"You, me, and whatever linked us up, man. We weren't alone. There was definitely something else in here."

"You stickin' around Seattle?"

"Got room?"

"Got floor."

"Okay then. I'll get my sleeping bag out of the car."

Eel glanced at Tommy and Abby.

"We're staying with a friend of Abby's mom."

"Plenty of floor if you want it," said Eel.

"Thanks. That's okay. I'm just glad you guys hit it off. That was incredible," said Tommy.

"We'll see if it happens twice," said Eel.

A few hours later, Eel grabbed his jacket and his guitar and headed for the door.

"I thought you didn't have a gig," said Squid.

"I don't. Just a job."

"So why are you taking the ax?"

"There's a lot of downtime."

"Want company?"

"I don't think the boss would approve. They don't know I play."

"Ahh. Okay. See you tomorrow then."

The first time Eel showed up at the aquarium with his guitar, the girl at the desk gave him a look, but since then no one seemed to notice. Each night he waited until all the day shift custodial staff had cleared out and after he had made his first round. Then he pulled a stool closer to the otter tank and played until his fingers ached.

The other otters seemed oblivious to the music, but Puki came alive. As soon as Eel touched the strings, the baby shot through the water toward the guitar, and twirled and somersaulted in place, batting the water with his paws whenever Eel stopped, as if encouraging him to play more. During those hours, Eel felt more at home than he had in months. He'd played before cheering crowds back in Virginia, but since coming out West he'd never had such an enthusiastic audience.

By morning, when the day janitor showed up, Eel had put away his guitar and was completely exhausted, yet strangely at peace and endowed with a patient willingness to follow this new path and see where it led.

The week after Callie's visit to the jail, the local papers featured some story about the cruise ship issue almost every day.

"Boy, Haven's all over the news. He must be pleased," said Celeste, peering over Callie's shoulder as she read the latest update.

Callie shrugged. "Yeah. He's happy."

Celeste pulled away and studied her sister. "But you're not."

"I didn't say that. I'm happy for him. And the cause. It's great. It's what we wanted." She paused. "It's what Haven wanted. He says this reporter seems to be really on board."

Celeste continued looking at her. "Uh huh."

Callie met her look and said, "Cut it out, Cele. Don't try to make something out of this. My boyfriend's in jail, and all's right with the world, okay? What's new in your life? How's it going with your Green Man?"

"Don't try to change the subject. You want to play it that way, I won't pry."

"Hah!"

"Okay. I'll restrain myself from prying until it gets unhealthy. You wouldn't want me to die of curiosity."

"There's just nothing to say. He's doing what he thinks is best. And I'm happy for him."

Celeste eyed her sister carefully. "Is there someone else?"

"For Haven?"

"No. For you. You seem distracted."

Callie opened her mouth to deny this charge, but shut it quickly. She didn't know how to describe the confusion that filled her mind every time she recalled Eel's voice or the way his eyes flashed green sparks when he talked about Puki.

"Callie? There's someone else?"

Callie pursed her lips.

Viola came into the kitchen and said, "Of course there's someone else. We saw him, remember? The guy with the green hair and the killer cheekbones."

"The guy that came to the bakery? Wow! Calliopsis! I take it all back. You do know how to live." Celeste's smile was as broad as her hips. Callie couldn't stop herself from smiling back.

"Okay. I've talked to him a few times. But there's nothing going on."

"Why not?" Celeste demanded. "Is he a drug dealer or something? I mean, is there some actual reason you wouldn't give him the time of day?"

"There's nothing specific. It's just... he's a slacker. He doesn't care about serious things."

Her sisters shared a look.

"Ah," said Celeste. "Well, don't you think it's your duty—"

"Your sacred duty," interrupted Viola.

"Thank you. Your sacred duty to educate him on the importance of the cause and save his soul?"

"Lead him to the light," added Viola, nudging Celeste with her elbow.

Callie tried to frown, but she knew her sisters could keep this up indefinitely, and she couldn't hold out against them. "Okay, okay."

"For the good of the cause," urged Celeste.

Callie nodded. "Exactly."

In the following days, while Haven's name became increasingly familiar to readers of the local news, Callie took to stopping by The Sounding more often, in the hope that she would run into Eel or someone who could give her a lead on where he'd gone. The weather was improving, the rains beginning to taper off, the sun shining longer on the lakes. Callie wandered around the university, where freshly minted greenery flickered in the canopy above the gothic brick buildings. She turned at every glancing shade of green, hoping it might be Eel, until she ran into him quite by chance at the U District Festival.

She was moving slowly up University Way amid the flip-flop wearing throngs when she heard a snatch of music that gave her chills on this rare, hot day. She edged closer, wriggling through the crowd until she saw the trio—guitar, keyboard and drums. Her eyes locked on the guitar player. He was singing a dark, droning ballad that rode on a swell of lush organ voicings. Eel had his eyes shut. She was staring at him, noticing the Celtic runes tattooed on his forearms, when he opened his eyes at the end of the song and looked right at her. He flashed her a grin. She turned, her only thought to get away. She needed time to collect herself. Her heart was beating much too fast.

Stymied in her escape by the dense crowd, she looked behind her to make sure he hadn't followed and discovered that, in fact, he had.

He smiled down at her. The sunlight caught in the fringe of his cropped hair made it shine like new grass. She felt strangely shy and at a loss for words, and since he seemed content to beam at her, they stood silent while the jostling crowd flowed around them.

"Were we that bad?" he asked.

"No! No. It was really good. You were really good... I was..."

"Surprised?"

She pressed her lips together before she answered. "A little. It wasn't what I expected."

Eel nodded. "'S a new band."

"You have a new band?"

"Yeah. Me and Squid—the little guy—we're just putting it together. We've only got a couple songs so far."

"Well, I liked it." Callie looked away, then turned back. "I'm glad things are going well for you."

He gave her a long look. "They could be better."

He stared into her eyes, and she forced herself to stare back as long as she could, but finally she laughed and said, "I didn't see you at the aquarium."

His eyebrows went up. "You looked for me?"

She smiled ruefully and first said, "No," then, "Yes."

He grinned. "I'm on the night shift now."

"Oh."

There was another pause, during which Callie tried unsuccessfully not to stare at him. It was unnerving how he stared back.

"I'm still keeping an eye on the kid," he said.

"That's good." Callie's throat felt too tight to say more. "Well, I won't keep you."

"You could."

Her eyes widened in spite of the sunshine.

"Keep me," he added. "If you wanted to."

She murmured, "I don't think so. I should go." She turned to walk away, but she heard him call after her, "Think about it."

And for the rest of the day, she did.

That night she dreamed of being out at sea, far from the sight of land, under a low sky of heavy, gray clouds. The sensation of being in the small dinghy was so strong, she could smell the salt air and feel the waves slapping against the boat. She sensed something in the water, a head bobbing nearby. She tried to see who it was, but the choppy waves blocked her view. At first she thought it was the baby otter, and she began to call it, but no sound came from her throat. She tried to raise her voice, to be heard above the wind and waves, but the view shifted, and she saw clearly Eel's face between the waves. He was in trouble, struggling to keep his head above the water. She tried to call out to him, but she was powerless to speak. She stood up in the boat, and suddenly she was awake, her heart pounding, sweat on her neck.

She lay back on the sheets, but it was a long time before she was able to fall asleep again.

In the morning, she could hardly keep her eyes open at the bakery. The Sunday morning pastry crowd had already come and gone, and she was hoping to retreat behind the proofing boxes for a breather, when the phone rang.

"It's your boyfriend," Celeste said, with a knowing look and one hand over the receiver.

Callie reached for the phone and managed to disguise her disappointment when she heard Haven's voice.

"Callie. Good news! I'm out, and we've got a court date!"

Callie slumped against the wall. "Oh. That's great. Isn't it?"

"Of course. It's what we wanted. Now if we can get cameras in the courtroom, we might really be able to get the message out."

"Yay."

There was a slight pause on the other end of the line. "You don't sound very excited."

"Of course I'm excited. I'm just a little tired. It's been—"

"Yes, I know this has been hard on you," Haven interrupted. "But I'm out now, and we can work together again. Can you come over tonight?"

Callie closed her eyes and tried to dredge up some enthusiasm. "Sure," she said. "That'd be great. I have exams this week, though."

"I just thought, if you come tonight we could go over the strategy for the trial, and I can bring you up to speed on our plans."

"Right. That would be good, I guess."

Another pause. "You guess? Callie, are you all right? Are you coming down with something? You don't sound like yourself. I can't afford to get sick right now. If you think you're contagious..."

"No, I'm... I'm not sick. I'm just tired. I haven't been sleeping well... since you've been in jail and everything."

"Well, you don't have to worry anymore. I'm back, and we've got lots of work to do." He paused again and continued in a different tone. "You know what? Maybe if you're that tired, it would be better for you to get a good night's sleep and come over tomorrow, after school. How's that sound?"

Callie sagged with relief. "I think that would be better. I'm just so exhausted right now, I can't think straight."

"That's fine. Don't worry about it. You rest up and we'll get back together tomorrow. I've got a lot of work I need to do tonight anyway."

"Okay. I'll see you tomorrow."

"Great. Can't wait."

"Yeah. Me too." Callie hung up and stared bleakly at the phone.

Celeste appeared from around the corner and said, "Um, not that it's any of my business, but you don't sound bubbling with joy to see your demon lover."

Callie frowned. "Him I'd like to see," she muttered.

Celeste raised her eyebrows.

Callie shook her head. "I don't know what's wrong with me. I've never felt like this before."

Celeste tilted her head. "Soooo, is this about Haven, or not?"

Callie put her head in her hands. "Oh God, Cele. I don't know. He thinks everything is the same as ever, but it's not. And I don't know if I even want it to be."

"And the reason for this would be...?"

Callie looked up at her with a rueful smile. "That would be my demon lover. My would-be demon lover, if you want to get technical."

"So you haven't..."

"No. I haven't."

"But you'd like to?"

"You know? I think I really would." She sighed heavily. "I should be feeling guilty. But I'm not. Except I feel guilty about not feeling guilty. I haven't done anything wrong. Yet. The thing is, I can't stop thinking about him, and I know I shouldn't be feeling like this, but I can't seem to care if it's wrong or not. It's wrong for me not to tell Haven how I feel. But he's so pumped right now about The Mission, and I don't want to upset him. He deserves a better girlfriend. Not somebody who would even consider what I've been considering."

"So you've been considering?"

Callie nodded. "Yeah. Big time. I wonder if this is how mom felt before she dove off the edge."

CHAPTER NINE

"Yes. Yes... exactly... Then you'll have the demonstrators there at ten thirty? Perfect...Thanks. Okay. Bye." Haven hung up the phone and inhaled with satisfaction before turning to Callie.

"Well. Everything's all set for our first day in court," he said, pacing back and forth.

"Good. I'm glad," she said, curling herself into a tight space on the couch. She waited to see if he was going to keep talking, but when he finally sat down it was on the chair in front of his computer. He quickly began clicking the mouse and tapping away. She sighed and looked out the window. A sun break was lighting up the new leaves on the chestnut trees lining the street outside, and Callie felt the call of the lake. It would be a perfect time to go for a row. On a weekday morning it wouldn't be crowded.

Haven was already absorbed at the computer. The patter of the keyboard sounded like footsteps running away. Callie wondered if he would even notice if she just slipped out. A shudder of disloyalty went through her. She shook it off. *This has nothing to do with loyalty*, she told herself.

And just what, exactly, is this about then? A memory of the way Eel's bristly green hair framed his pale face hit her, and she swallowed hard. *Yeah. That's what this is about.*

"Callie? Are you listening to me?"

She looked up and realized that Haven had turned around and was staring at her with concern. "Are you all right? I was asking if you want to read this copy of the Maritime Journal report on the dangers of cruise ship traffic in the Sound."

She wrenched her thoughts away from Eel and smiled brightly. "You know? I really think I need some fresh air. I've been cooped up at work and school for days and... I just need to get outside."

Haven nodded. "Okay. Maybe that's a good idea. We can take a walk and I'll fill you in on the gist of the story. We can go over the plan for tomorrow." He stood up and stretched. "Probably do me good to get out and get some exercise too. After all, I was locked up for a week."

"That must have been awful."

"It wasn't so bad. I only had to share the cell with one guy, and he was in there for breaking into an ATM machine with a crowbar, so we got along all right."

He started putting on a jacket. "And Sandra came to talk almost every day, so the time was well spent. I don't think she would have been able to give the story the space it deserves if I hadn't stayed in jail."

"That's great. I mean... that she came every day." Callie slipped into her hoodie and stood by the door.

Haven came up beside her and said in a proprietary tone as he put his arm around her shoulders, "You have nothing to worry about Calliekins. She was only doing her job."

"Of course. I know that." She slipped under his arm and out the door, hoping he would think she hadn't noticed the unspoken kiss op which had just passed. She simply couldn't pretend to be in the mood.

They walked briskly down the block and marched their usual route along Ravenna Avenue toward the lake. By the time they got there, Callie had decided against asking Haven to go for a boat ride. She didn't want to be stuck in a small space with him. She knew there would be no chance of enjoying the peace and calm out on the water with his running monologue in her ear.

They set off on the three-mile walk around the lake, and Callie was able to give the appearance of listening by filling in with an occasional 'oh really?' or 'that's true' whenever he glanced at her. Haven appeared satisfied with these tokens of attention. He was so accustomed to Callie's agreement that he scarcely noticed the absence of passion in her comments.

She concentrated on the changing colors of the shoreline, where the grays of late winter were disappearing beneath vernal growth. A new crop of coots and ducks paddled the silvery surface of the lake, darting in and out of the shadows. The energy of early spring, the quickening pulse of earth and sky reflected at the water's edge, gave her a kind of contact high. She glanced at Haven droning on, seemingly unaware of where he was, and felt a stab of pity at the thought of hurting him. He didn't deserve that. He turned and caught her looking at him and smiled.

"It's nice to see you smiling," he said.

"Am I? I didn't even know," she said, struggling to maintain her smile under his earnest gaze. "It's just so nice to be out here."

He nodded absently. "Yes. It's pleasant. Come on. I need to get back before three. I'm expecting a fax."

Callie followed as he set off in an easterly direction at a faster pace. He resumed talking, while Callie admired the cherry trees budding by the soccer field.

"Callie? Are you listening?"

She paused, mid-step, and looked at him. "Of course I'm listening. It's what I do."

He frowned slightly. "I thought you'd want to know. I thought you might even possibly have a suggestion."

Callie bit her tongue to stop the retort that leapt to it. "I'm sorry," she said. "I was distracted. What were you saying?"

In a somewhat mollified tone Haven said, "I was saying it's too bad we don't have a mascot."

"A what? You mean like the Mariner Moose?"

"No. Not exactly. Sandra's faxing me a possible logo for the story—some visual cue to help readers follow it. Their art department was working up something with seals, I think. Sandra said the best thing would be if we had a photogenic mascot, like a baby seal, we could give it a name, like Sammy the Seal, and then kids would get interested and their parents would follow."

"So... you're looking for something like Smokey the Bear?"

"That's the idea. The trouble is, we need it right now. Ideally it would be an animal that had to be rescued because the increased ship traffic in the Sound has made it too dangerous."

"Hmm," said Callie, her eyes glued to the sidewalk. "Yeah, that's a tough one."

"The logo will probably be fine. Sandra's just trying to give the story every advantage. I think she really understands what's at stake."

Callie glanced at his face. His eyes were focused far away, somewhere in the future, perhaps. "Well, that's great," she said. "I'm glad she's in your corner."

They had reached Haven's block. "Do you want to come up?" he asked.

"Um, I don't think so. I have a lot of work to do too."

Haven nodded. "It's probably better. Sandra's going to call, and we'll be going over the strategy for tomorrow. Are you coming to watch?"

"I really can't. Besides, it's going to be so crowded and you'll be busy and—"

"It's okay. You don't have to be there." He smiled. "You can read about me in the news!"

She nodded with a little smile. "Yeah. I'll do that."

He kissed her lightly on the cheek and trotted off toward his building.

Callie looked at her watch. It wasn't even three o'clock. She glanced up at the blue sky peeking between the scudding white clouds. The Sounding would be open for another couple of hours. In her mind she tiptoed around the ledge of the chasmic lie of omission she had just told Haven. A photogenic mascot for the cause? Why couldn't she tell him about Puki? Why did every fiber of her being resist sharing her 'baby' with Haven and his media connections?

There was only one person she wanted to share Puki with. She got on a bus and headed to the waterfront.

The line outside The Sounding surprised her. Usually on a weekday things weren't so crowded, unless it was summer. Or unless... she looked out behind the building and saw the shadow of one of the smaller cruise ships.

When she got inside, it took her a while to work her way past the clusters of children and retirees gawking at the octopus tanks and jellyfish displays. At the end of the dark passageway that led to the otter zone, a bright yellow sign stopped her in her tracks:

OUT SICK
Puki, our baby sea otter, has been
temporarily removed from the otter
tank due to illness. He'll be back
as soon as he recovers!

Callie stared at the sign, breathing shallowly, her mind racing. She went to find someone in the office.

There was no one at a desk who could talk to her, and it took a while to find someone who would tell her the whole story. She eventually cornered Marybeth Swenson, one of the long-time volunteers who had been there the day she brought in Puki. She told Callie that Eel had been put on leave, pending an inquiry into Puki's behavior. Apparently a change had come over the baby since Eel began working nights. Puki had become listless and was refusing food, though he had no other symptoms of illness.

Eel had been singled out because of the damning testimony of an anonymous source at one of The Sounding's major donors. Marybeth said someone claimed to have seen Eel giving drugs to the little otter after hours.

Callie was shocked and outraged. She knew Eel would never do such a thing. But she understood that the aquarium had to investigate such a serious charge.

"He must be miserable," she said.

"No. They said he seems fine. He just won't eat. And he's not as playful as he used to be," said Marybeth.

"I meant Eel."

"Oh." Marybeth looked at her. "I suppose so. He seemed like a nice young man."

"He is! I can't believe he would have done this." Callie took a deep breath. "Do you know? I guess you wouldn't. I wonder how I could find him."

"Which one? Puki, or the young man?"

"Both. I'd really like to talk with Eel. But I don't know where he lives. Do you think they would give me his phone number? They must have it here."

"I'm sure we can find it," Marybeth said.

Moments later Callie left with a scrap of paper on which was scribbled Eel's address. They couldn't find a phone number.

She stood outside the low-rise apartment building just north of the U District and studied the windows, trying to guess which one might be Eel's. She realized he might not have a window facing the street at all. She knew she was hesitating because... well, this was it. If she went in and knocked on his door, he would know. He would know, even if the only things they talked about were Puki and politics. He would know. And she could already imagine the light in his eyes when he saw her at his door, because... he would know.

She decided, stepping lightly to the entrance, it was about time.

Eel was lying on the couch with a cigarette, watching the smoke curling toward the crack in the plaster ceiling and trying not to think about anything, much less the cracked state of his current existence, when a soft knock at the door set all his nerves on edge.

This knock was none that he recognized, and, by a swift process of deduction, Eel guessed the one person who might be likely, even in this mostly cracked world, to come to his door. Thus, when he opened it and saw her there, his smile might have seemed out of context for a man whose life at the moment was one swing ahead of the wrecking ball.

"Hello," he said.

"Hi. I know you must be surprised to see me."

"Not really. I mean, yes. But..." He took a breath. "Can you come in?"

She stepped in, took a quick glance around the almost empty room, and noticed the cigarette. "You really need to stop those."

He stubbed it out against the door frame and said, "Yeah. I did. This was just a bit of back sliding. 'S a bad habit. I been... had a bit to think about." He shrugged. "Hey, I got a couch. It was out on the curb. Me and Squid lugged it up the stairs. You can sit there, if you want."

"Okay." She gave a little laugh and went over and sat on the couch. She looked back at him. "Aren't you going to sit down?"

"Thought I'd guard the door." He stared at her. "You look good on that."

She shook her head. "I went by to see Puki and—"

"I didn't do it."

"I know that. I knew that. I wanted to see you because there's got to be a way to prove that you're innocent, and I thought maybe I could help."

Eel's stare grew more intense. "Really?"

"Really," she said, staring back until a blush began to creep across her pale cheeks.

He came over and sat down beside her. "I'd never hurt him."

"I know."

"He's like..." He looked at the bare floor. "He's like a kid." He looked up into her eyes. "Your kid. My kid. Only he's... special."

"Yeah," Callie breathed. "That's how I feel. Exactly."

"I think I know who framed me."

"Who?"

"I caught some guy harassing the kid when I worked one of those parties. Guy was a real jerk. Didn't like being told off by the janitor in front of his girlfriend. The kind of petty creep who'd want to get me fired."

"But even if that's true, what's wrong with Puki?"

Eel shook his head. "I don't know. They wouldn't let me see him. They said I'd have to wait till they run some tests." He frowned. "He was fine when he was with me. I played guitar for him every night. He loved it. He's my best fan ever."

"Really?" Callie grinned. "That is so sweet! I wish I could have seen it."

Eel nodded. "It's pretty great. He does these flips. When he's happy."

"I'll talk to them. I'll explain. If we can find out who accused you, we can figure out how to fight back."

Eel smiled at her.

"What?" she said.

He shrugged. "So now you're fighting for me?"

Callie gave him a look. "I just don't think it's fair to go around accusing people of doing things without any proof."

"So you'd fight for anyone, then?"

She tried not to smile. "Maybe not anyone."

"And this has nothing to do with you and me?"

A shadow flitted across her face. "I... I'm still technically Haven's girlfriend."

"Whoa. 'Technically?' What does that mean?"

Callie sighed. "It means... it means I haven't said anything to him. But... I think I have to."

"Really?" Eel waited. Callie kept silent. Eel's knee began twitching. He got up and paced by the window overlooking the street.

"I should go," said Callie.

"You just got here."

"I know but... technically... I shouldn't have come at all."

Eel snorted. "Why not? We're friends, right? You're allowed to have friends aren't you? Technically?"

Callie stood and came close to him. She looked steadily in his eyes and said quietly, "The trouble is, I don't want to be just friends." And with that, she turned and went out the door before Eel could recover himself enough to respond.

CHAPTER TEN

After a front page start, the newspaper coverage of Haven's case lost out to flashier headlines as the trial bogged down in judicial maneuvering. By the end of the week, the cruise ship protest story amounted to four column inches buried on page three of the City section.

Meanwhile, the investigation of Puki's lassitude reached a turning point when the blood work results came back with a clean bill of health and no evidence of any drugs in his system. Callie was jubilant until she called to ask about Eel's job.

"I'm sorry, Callie," said the aquarium director. "I understand Eel's your friend, but until we know for sure what's causing the change in Puki, we can't make any decisions. We can't rush the process."

"But that's not fair to Eel. First you accuse him of a really horrible thing, which he would never do, and then you won't even clear his record when the evidence shows he's innocent?"

"Callie, please. We're trying to be fair. Puki is very important to all of us, including our sponsors. They expect us to be diligent in protecting all the creatures in our care, and we need to be certain that the change in Puki's condition was not caused by any action of Eel's."

"What do you mean?"

"There have been suggestions that Eel may been disrupting Puki's normal routine."

"What are you talking about?"

"It's been brought to our attention that Eel was in the habit of playing his electric guitar near the otter habitat. It's possible that, while his intentions may have been good, the impact of that might be the root cause of Puki's malaise."

"That's ridiculous! Eel told me Puki loved it when he played."

"Maybe so. I'm simply saying, we can't allow Eel back until we've established what's causing Puki to refuse food. If then."

"What does that mean?"

"Callie, we'll just have to see. I know you're especially fond of Puki because you were responsible for his rescue, but he's under our care now, and you must trust us to do what's best for him."

"What if I don't?"

"Callie. You're upset—"

"Can't you see how wrong you are? You're not giving Eel a chance to tell his side. He knows Puki as well as—better than anyone. You should at least let him come in and see Puki. He cares about him, and he's really worried."

In the background Callie heard the bubbling of the water filters in the tanks near the office. The director let out a long breath and said, "All right. That's fair. We'll allow Eel to visit Puki at the infirmary, and we'll observe the effect. But I'm not making any promises."

"Okay. Thank you. I'll tell him, and call you to arrange a time."

"And Callie?"

"Yes?"

"Make it soon. We've got to get to the bottom of this before the summer season gets into high gear. Puki is one of our stars."

Callie hung up in a pensive mood. Sure, it was something that they'd agreed to let Eel see Puki. But she didn't like the way the director talked about the pup. It reminded her of Haven's plea.

Everyone wanted to exploit the cute otter, supposedly for his own good, and that didn't sit right with her.

At the edge of a small pool bathed in milky green light filtered through translucent panels above, Eel stood with his guitar. The air was damp and cool, and smelled of seaweed and raw fish. The aquarium director, Callie, and a half dozen marine biologists were gathered in the narrow space between the pool and the wall.

Puki and two older otters were swimming around, seemingly oblivious to the humans.

Eel flipped the standby switch on his practice amp and began to play softly. All eyes were on Puki.

At the sound of the first note, the baby otter stopped swimming and turned his head toward Eel. He hovered in the water for a few seconds, then dove under the surface and out of sight. The scientists murmured among themselves until Puki popped up a few feet from Eel and slapped the water with his paws. His eyes were shining and a funny little grin spread below his whiskers. Eel grinned back at him, and Puki responded with a series of quick backflips before returning to treading water in front of Eel.

Eel kept playing. The melody was unlike the droning piece Callie had heard him play at the festival. It was more lyrical and expressive, with circles of notes that rose and fell and repeated in waves of harmony. The soft music resonated in the chamber like the tolling of a buoy out at sea.

Puki continued to flip and twirl, slapping the water repeatedly and making little chuckling noises. When the song ended, Puki slapped the water more vigorously, his head bobbing at Eel.

Eel turned to the staff. "He always liked that one," he said.

"Keep playing," said one of the scientists.

Eel began another song, a lively tune like a Celtic hornpipe. Puki reacted with antic joy, somersaulting and kicking his feet, floating on his back and clapping his paws. The other otters ignored the music.

When Eel stopped again, Puki swam right up to him and grabbed the lip of the pool with his paws, tilting his head at Eel expectantly.

One of the scientists muttered, "Wait a minute. I want to try something." He hurried out of the room and returned a moment later with a bucket of raw abalone chunks, the kind that were fed to all the otters at the aquarium several times a day.

"Can you put your guitar away for a minute?" he asked Eel. "I want to see if he'll accept food from you. We haven't had much success getting him to eat since he came here."

Eel took the bucket and said, "I just toss it to him, right?"

"Right. Anywhere near him is fine."

Eel looked at Puki and said, "Okay, kid. You must be hungry." He took a piece of fish and tossed it toward Puki.

Puki grabbed it and stuffed it in his mouth. Then he floated on his back, eyeing Eel. Eel threw another piece. Puki eagerly caught it and gobbled it.

Eel looked at the scientist who had handed him the bucket.

"What do you think?" asked Eel. "Can I give him the rest?"

The scientist smiled. "I think you better. It's obvious he's bonded with you."

"Well, that's good isn't it?" asked Callie. "So there's nothing wrong with him, except he loves Eel?"

"Looks that way," said the scientist.

While Eel continued tossing fish to the voracious Puki, he caught the director's eye and asked, "Does this mean I can have my job back?"

"Actually, Eel, I'd like to put you back on the day shift, so you can take charge of feeding Puki. How would you feel about that? You'd have to feed him during visitor demonstrations."

"Would I have to talk to the tourists?"

"One of the volunteers can do that."

"Okay then. I'm your man."

"Looks like you're Puki's man, now," said Callie.

81

Eel gave her a look. "How do you feel about joint custody?"

She closed the distance between them and said quietly, "We have to talk."

A short while later Callie and Eel were back on the street, walking to his car, Callie with her hands in the pockets of her hoodie, Eel holding his guitar and amp. They walked in silence. Callie kept smiling as she recalled how Eel had looked tossing fish to Puki, and how magical it had seemed, as if Puki knew that Eel belonged to him. Now, strolling beside Eel in the late afternoon, with spring lighting up the clouds, Callie had a feeling that he belonged to her too. And she was far too happy to feel guilty.

"You said you wanted to talk?" Eel kept walking as he spoke, not looking at her.

She shook her head. "I say a lot of stupid stuff."

"No you don't." He stopped and turned to her, and the look on his face left her breathless.

When she didn't reply, he resumed walking. She slipped her arm through his and fell into step beside him.

"Hey. They've got a picture of your baby in the paper!" Celeste leaned back in her chair and glanced over at Callie, who was buttering a muffin at the counter.

"What?" Callie bent to read the photo caption: "The Sounding's newest attraction, 'Puki', a baby sea otter, enjoys a morning snack in the water."

She skimmed the rest of the article, which told how Puki had been rescued by a local resident (it didn't mention her name, Callie noticed with relief), and how he had developed a special attachment to one of the employees, who was a musician.

Callie pursed her lips.

"What's the matter?" Celeste asked. "I thought you'd be pleased. It's a really cute picture."

Callie took a bite of her muffin and chewed for a moment. "Otters are just intrinsically photogenic. I mean, you know—the whiskers, the button eyes. The thing is, I'm a little worried that this woman at the aquarium wants to use Puki as a marketing tool."

Celeste shrugged. "Well, duh. I'm sure they need money. They gotta do what they gotta do."

"Yeah but," Callie stared at the photo. Maybe she was being unreasonable. Maybe it wouldn't hurt to generate more support for the aquarium. She had to stop being so paranoid.

"Maybe you're right," she said. "It is a cute picture."

"So, you and the demon lover? How's that working out? You got a 'special attachment' too?" Celeste put down the paper and grinned at Callie.

Callie frowned. "Maybe. But you won't be reading about it in the paper."

"I should hope not. Haven should hear it from you first."

"Oh hell." Callie sat down at the table and rested her head in her hands. "He's gonna see that picture."

"So?"

"He was talking to me the other day about how what his case needs is a good PR symbol, something the newspapers can use like a logo to catch the public eye and win their hearts and minds, so to speak."

"Ah. Like a cute, orphaned baby otter."

"Right."

"And, let me guess... you didn't mention that you had just the thing he needed."

Callie shook her head. "I haven't even told him I found Puki. I was going to, at first. But then he went to jail, and all this court stuff started. He's been so wrapped up in that. He just didn't seem interested in my... in what I was doing."

"Hmmm. So, when Haven figures out that you didn't tell him, I wonder how he's going to react?"

Callie leaned back in her chair, feeling slightly queasy. "Should I tell him now?"

Celeste shrugged. "It's probably too late now. If I were you, I'd work on my plausible excuse."

Callie stared out the window. "Puki was in the infirmary. They thought Eel had given him drugs. I could say that I thought the timing was wrong. Or something like that."

"Eel was giving him drugs?"

"Of course not. He was playing guitar for him. At night. And Puki loved it. He's crazy about music. You should see it." Callie smiled at the memory of Puki and Eel. Then she caught the look in Celeste's eye and stopped smiling.

Celeste shook her head. "Sounds to me like there's a lot of stuff you haven't been telling Haven. Not that I care. But..."

"Yeah, I know. I need to talk to him. I've just been waiting for the right time. He's so busy with the cruise ship thing, and I hate to upset him."

Celeste stood up. "Well, you better tell him soon. Before he reads about you in the papers."

"Shoot."

Celeste patted her on the shoulder. "Ah, don't worry Calliope. It might not be that bad. Haven's a big boy. He can handle a little disappointment. You'll probably just get a lecture. And maybe have to stay after class." Celeste giggled as she left the room.

"Oh crap," Callie muttered, and dropped her head to the table.

When Callie came out of class a few hours later, her heart sank at the sight of a familiar silhouette leaning against the bike racks. She briefly considered trying to slip back in the building and sneak out the other exit, even though it would only delay the inevitable. She had been daydreaming about Eel during the last half-hour in class. A confrontation with Haven was the last thing she wanted.

Before she could shift into reverse, Haven turned and looked her right in the eye. She couldn't pretend she hadn't seen him. When he lifted a copy of the morning paper and waggled it toward her with a quizzical look, Callie braced for the cross examination. As he got closer, though, it seemed to her that his usual air of invulnerable composure was slightly off, as if he'd been shaken, not stirred.

In three long strides he was next to her. "Callie? Have you seen this morning's paper?"

She attempted a look of innocence. "I didn't have time to look at it this morning."

"So you didn't see this?" He held out the paper, folded to display the photo of Puki.

"Gosh, no," she lied. "That's a cute picture."

Haven frowned slightly. He folded his arms in front of his chest and said, "So, you didn't know about this orphaned otter when we were having our conversation the other day about a signature image for the campaign?"

Callie hesitated. There was nothing unusual about Haven's calm, overbearing manner, but it was the first time he'd used it on her, and she was amazed at how irritating it was. She bristled and replied, "Okay. Yes, I knew about Puki. But I didn't say anything because he was under observation in the infirmary at the time, and I didn't think it would be good to complicate things with a lot of publicity."

"Hmm," Haven responded, nodding. "So, you were waiting..."

"What is this, the third degree? I would have told you when the time was right."

Haven nodded stiffly. "I see. Well, no harm done. I'm pleased to report that I spoke with one of the administrators at The Sounding this morning and outlined the situation with our case, and she was very helpful. She said they would be happy to let us use a photo of the otter for our logo." He smiled condescendingly and patted her on the back. "I understand that you were trying to do what you thought best, but you should have told me right away when you learned they had a baby otter. It's a real stroke of luck for us. And an orphan too. The woman I talked to said its mother was killed by a boat, so that's a nice touch. Sandra said it was perfect."

Callie gaped at him as he went on enthusiastically detailing how the campaign would include full page ads in the papers, posters on buses and billboards around town. The tiny moment of relief Callie had felt when she realized Haven didn't know she was the one who had found the baby otter in the first place was dwarfed by her growing sense of outrage at how he planned to exploit her baby. When he paused and looked at her as if expecting her congratulations, she sputtered momentarily before she managed to put her fury into words.

"So you've got it all figured out, huh? And how convenient that his mother was killed, just for you!"

Haven lowered his voice and said, "Callie. Why are you talking like this?"

"Maybe because I actually care about Puki! He's a sweet little baby, and you want to put him in the spotlight and make him do tricks for the cameras. You don't need him to win your case. Why can't you just leave him alone?"

"Callie, there's no need to be hysterical. I told you. Sandra says with a big story like this it's vital to have something symbolic for the public to focus on. And this baby otter is just the thing. We won't hurt him. We want to preserve his natural habitat. You know that."

"I know that once Puki becomes famous nobody is ever going to let him return to his natural habitat. He'll be a prisoner of the corporate media machine, trapped in that little tank for life."

"Callie. What's come over you? This otter is only a symbol of our larger fight. He's a little soldier in the war to save the oceans. Surely you of all people can understand that."

Callie glared at him. She took a few calming breaths and continued in a lower tone. "Of course I understand what we're fighting for. But we don't agree on the methods. It's one thing for you to go to jail willingly to make your point. It's entirely different to take a wild animal and turn him into a cartoon mascot."

"Don't be ridiculous. What about Smokey the Bear? He was a real bear, orphaned by real fires, and he became a universally recognized symbol of fire prevention."

Callie glowered. "Yeah. And that worked out real well didn't it? Tell it to San Diego."

Haven took a step back. "Honestly, Callie, I thought you understood. Why are you being like this? Is it that time of the month?"

"How dare you! Is it that time of the month when you act like a pompous jackass? I guess so!"

Haven lowered his voice and tucked the paper under his arm. "Maybe I should go. You obviously need time to control your emotions."

"What would you know about emotions?"

"I'll talk to you when you've calmed down." He turned and walked away. Callie fought the urge to throw something at him. That, she knew, would only make him feel even more superior. She kicked the curb instead and slouched off in the opposite direction.

She had been walking only a few minutes, muttering angry arguments she wished she'd had the presence of mind to use with Haven, when she realized that, unconsciously, she was walking toward downtown, the docks, The Sounding. Eel would be there. Puki would be there. She quickened her pace.

CHAPTER ELEVEN

The first thing she noticed was the noise.

Usually, down along the waterfront, the constant rumble of traffic drowned out the seaside soundtrack of gulls, waves and ferry horns. But today there was another element in the mix—a buzzing murmur like the echoing chatter of an audience before a concert. It grew louder as Callie got closer to The Sounding.

Hundreds of people were milling around the entrance. Callie tried to push through to the door, but the crowd was too dense and determined. When she attempted to get past a sunburned woman who was gripping the hand of a small boy wearing a Dallas Cowboys cap and a scowl, the woman snapped, "Hey, we were here first! Wait your turn!"

The air was thick with the scent of popcorn, taffy, and sweat. Callie nearly gagged as she wormed her way out of the crowd and back to the fresh air on the nearby pier. She slumped onto one of the benches. A pair of seagulls promptly landed at her feet and cocked their heads in her direction.

"Sorry. If you want popcorn, you better try next door," she muttered, glaring back at the crowd.

The sun was warm, and the sky was the bright, cloudless blue that graces Seattle for three fleeting months each year. Ordinarily, Callie would have basked in the sheer beauty of the day, but the clamor in front of the aquarium destroyed any hope of serenity. She imagined what it must be like inside, where the observation areas and halls were designed to accommodate a modest, steady flow of visitors. Callie shuddered to think how loud it must be. At least Puki could escape the noise by going underwater. Eel would have no way out.

She waited nearly an hour, hoping the crowd would diminish enough to allow her to get to the door, but if anything, the crush seemed to grow, spilling out over the sidewalk. One of the panhandlers who had been circling closer finally dropped onto the bench beside her and said, "You got a boyfriend?" Callie smiled tightly and said, "Yes." Then she got up and walked to the nearest bus stop. Enough was enough, and too much was definitely too much.

She was settling down on the couch with a cup of tea and a textbook, hoping to focus on her studies for an hour or two, when a soft knock set Rugby barking.

"Hush," she murmured, shuffling to the door, expecting to see a Sierra Club volunteer or the like.

Her jaw dropped when she saw Eel.

"How did you find where I live?" she asked.

"I went to the bakery first. Your sisters said you'd be here."

"Come in. I went by the aquarium today to see you, but I couldn't get in."

He followed her into the living room, and sank onto the couch. "I kept thinking it would let up. Never did."

"Was it awful?"

He leaned forward and looked at her with an air of sadness that surprised her. "We've got to get him out of there," he said quietly.

"Puki?"

"Yeah! 'S like..." He frowned at the floor. "'S like, I used to think it was a nice place... nice enough anyway... you know? Kind of dark and quiet, and they seem happy enough, swimming around and playing with their toys and stuff. But today—people were reaching into the tank and trying to grab him. One kid got bit—not by Puki—but they wouldn't listen. And the ones who wanted to hear couldn't anyway because of all the shrieking and yakking—cell phones! People taking pictures with their freakin' cell phones. I kept waiting for somebody to drop one in the tank. It was a freakin' zoo. And I don't mean the animals."

Callie shook her head. "It can't stay like this. The crowds are bound to go down."

"Why? Why would people stop coming? And they wanna make it worse. Ms. Anderson and all the rest of them. They were like high at the end of the day, so happy about the big turnout and the publicity. And it's only just started. Did you know they're gonna put pictures of him on buses? And billboards? They're gonna run ads in magazines, and someone from the Travel Channel wants to do a bit on the otters for their show on Seattle."

"Gosh."

"Yeah."

"I mean, I guess I can understand why Ms. Anderson is excited. The money's going to be rolling in, and that's good. But..."

"Yeah. But. But you and me are the only ones who give a crap about Puki. Everybody else just wants to sell him to the highest bidder. You watch—they'll be pitching him to the talk shows."

"Oh God, no! He's just a baby."

"They don't care." Eel studied her face before reaching for her hand. "They want me to start playing my songs during the demos, to make Puki go nuts for the crowds." He ran his fingers over the back of her hand as he looked into her eyes. "I'm not gonna do that. But I'm afraid if I don't, they'll find somebody else to play for him. I shouldn't care, but..."

Callie put her other hand over Eel's and squeezed it gently. "They don't understand. He's not some circus animal. He's a magical creature."

"What can we do?"

Holding his hand, Callie tried to see a way out of the situation. There was nothing to stop the aquarium from going ahead with its marketing plans. But the more she thought about her own role in putting Puki into what now seemed to her a trap, she couldn't let it continue. She looked deep into Eel's eyes and said, "I think you're right. We've got to get him out of there."

"Won't be easy. Where can we take him?"

Callie kept a tight grip on his hand while she thought furiously.

"We've got to let him go."

"You mean, back to the sea?"

"Yes. It's where he belongs. Free."

"But can he make it on his own? Isn't he too little still? I thought that was the reason you took him to the aquarium in the first place."

"That was two months ago. He's stronger now, and bigger. And besides, we won't just throw him into the Sound alone. We'll find a raft of otters out in the sea and release him next to them. They'll take him in."

"Are you sure?"

"It's their nature. They gather in groups to sleep together, floating on their backs. Sometimes they hold hands while they sleep. And they tie themselves together with strands of kelp so they won't drift apart."

"You're kidding."

"No. It's true. They have this amazing social network. All we have to do is find a group for Puki to join."

"Sounds too easy."

"We'll need to be careful. And we'll have to do some exploring first. Once we get him out of the aquarium, we'll have to move really fast."

Eel stared at her. "You really think we can do it?"

She took a deep breath and let it out slowly. "I don't know. But we've got to try."

Eel pulled her close and held her. She closed her eyes and surrendered to the moment she'd been longing for since he walked through the door.

After he left, Callie shed her air of confidence. The task of freeing Puki would be *Mission-Impossible* tricky, and without a lot of luck they could make things even worse for the baby otter. As Callie pondered the obstacles ahead, she realized that if they were to have any hope of success, they would need the help of someone who knew the sea far better than she did.

She glanced at the clock, grabbed her jacket, and headed out.

She found him sitting on the back porch, smoking his pipe, stroking a gray cat, and staring at the gulls wheeling above the shipyard next to the Ballard Bridge. The sun had dropped behind Magnolia, but brightness reflected off the water lit the air.

He was wearing the same battered captain's cap he'd worn six days a week during the forty years he'd taken his fishing boat out on the Sound. Now he had sold the boat and no longer fished, but Stephan Linden still read the sea like a book, with the pages earmarked at his favorite passages.

Callie slipped onto the folding chair next to him and reached over to pet the cat. Her grandfather took the pipe from his mouth. "You didn't come here to visit Lucy now, did you?" he asked.

"No." Callie rocked on her chair and eyed him cautiously before she asked, "Grandpa, what do you know about sea otters?"

"Everything."

She grinned. "I thought so."

"What do you want to know?"

She stopped grinning. "Is it possible to return an otter to the sea... if it was rescued as a baby and kept in an aquarium?"

Stephan raised an eyebrow. "Are we talking about a particular otter?"

"Yes."

"And why would you be wanting to return this otter to the sea?"

"Because... because I'm the one that found him. His mother was dead. And I took him to The Sounding because I didn't know what else to do. But now they're... they want to use him for their advertising... and I don't think it's right for Puki to have to be a mascot for the rest of his life."

"Puki?"

Callie nodded.

Stephan scratched his silver beard and looked out at the shipyard. "So this is something you want to do... and the people who have the otter now..."

"They wouldn't agree if I asked them."

"So you won't be asking them?"

"Right."

Stephan nodded and continued to stroke the cat. After a while he said, "It's not easy to put a wild thing back in the wild. And if it's a young'un..." He squinted at Callie. "You've thought about this? You think it's the best thing for the creature? You've thought about how much trouble you'll be in when it comes out what you've done?"

Callie met his eyes, which were gray and deep like the Sound.

"I know it's crazy. But I'm responsible for Puki being there, and I just can't let them use him like this."

"Even if it's for a good cause?"

"They don't need to exploit him to make money. They've got other otters who were born and raised in the aquarium. They can use one of those. But Puki—he's special... he's... not like the others. And he really cares about... this guy I know... and we want to set him free."

Stephan nodded. "So you have someone to help you?"

"Yes."

Stephan nodded again. "That's good. When the going gets rough, it's good to have someone at your side."

"I've got you."

For a second Callie thought the old man was going to smile, but a graver expression settled on his face. "I can't help you with this."

Callie sat back in her chair. "I know. But can you tell us where to take him, to let him go?"

Stephan straightened up and set the cat on the porch. "I can't tell you exactly. There haven't been any sea otters in the Sound for as long as I can remember. But I can show you on the map where to look." He stood up and opened the door for Callie. She walked in, and he followed, going to the large oak table and pulling down a chart from a nearby shelf. He unrolled the chart and pointed to a section of the Strait of Juan de Fuca. "This would be a good place to start. A few years back there was a bunch of them living around Neah Bay. Could be they're moving eastward."

Stephan lifted his gaze from the map and said, "You'll have to go by yourself first—to find them."

"Can't Eel come with me?"

"That's your friend?"

"Yes."

"Interesting name." He paused to fetch his pipe before continuing. "The otters might show themselves if your friend comes along. But they might not. If you're alone, they'll come."

"How do you know?"

The lines on Stephan's face curved with his smile. "Because it's you, Callie girl. They'll know you. Like they knew your mother."

Callie held her breath, staring at her grandfather, willing him to say more, while the air between them shimmered with unspoken truths. Her grandfather reached out his hand and tapped her chest, just above her heart, with one finger. "It's in there, girl. You know it's true. If you go out and listen to the sea, it'll tell you where to find them."

"And if I do?"

"Then you'll know where to take your Puki."

"And they'll take care of him?"

"He's one of them, isn't he? Listen to your heart. Trust the sea."

Callie hadn't planned to tell Eel before she went on her otter-finding mission, but when he called that night and asked if they could search together, she found she couldn't lie to him, and Eel balked.

"Alone? Why? I could help. Don't you want me to come?"

"Yes."

"Is that a yes, you want me to come, or a yes, you don't?"

"I'd like you to come. But Grandpa said the otters might not come to me unless I'm alone."

"Why would they come to you anyway?"

Callie struggled to find words that wouldn't sound totally insane. "My grandpa has always told me, ever since I was a little girl, that I have... a gift... for the sea. And he says the otters know that. And they'll come to me."

She held onto the phone as if it were the tie line to her ship of dreams. If he laughed at her now, she would have to let go.

After a long pause he said, "And you believe this?"

She sighed. "I don't know. When I was a little girl my mom always called me her little mermaid. I know it was just a name, but... didn't you ever wish you could talk to animals or fly or do something impossible?"

There was a longer pause. "You think you're a mermaid?"

"No. Maybe. Not really. But I do feel more at home on water than on land. I don't know why." She snorted softly. "It's just a thing. All my life I've never been like other girls. And my mother was... different. She was... well... I guess she was probably nuts. She told me she was a mermaid, and she would tell me crazy stories about her life underwater. And then, when I was five years old, she left and never came back. But my Grandpa says she had the gift, and he says I do too."

"All right. So you have a gift. I'll buy it. But I still think I should come along. I can help. I got gifts. Ask anybody."

"Oh really?"

"I could take my acoustic. We could play a few tunes. I can see 'em now. All those otters, waving their little lighters, asking for an encore."

"You can come next time, okay? When we set him free. I'll need your help then."

The silence that followed lasted so long she was about to ask if he was still there when he said, "Call me when you get back?"

"I will," she promised.

CHAPTER TWELVE

The next morning a lone green kayak slipped between the bobbing waves like a grain of rice floating in a bowl of salty soup.

Callie had been paddling for a solid hour, skirting the western coast of Whidbey Island, scanning the surface of the sea, looking for signs of otters.

So far, the only wildlife she had come across was a lone orca that circled her boat a couple of times before swimming out of sight. Orcas, who had seldom bothered sea otters in the past, had recently been driven to eating them in areas where their usual prey had been decimated by environmental degradation and over-fishing. Callie watched the orca disappear. In spite of the warm sunshine playing on the water, she felt chilled at the thought of putting Puki in the open sea. Once they let him go, there would be no way to know what happened to him.

She raised the paddle and rested it on the hull, turning to gauge how far she was from the shore. The island cliffs rose in a golden sweep above the water. She remembered hiking along those cliffs with her father when she was a young girl, before she'd learned to sail a boat. The sea had seemed like an endless space to her then. Now it didn't seem so infinite. She knew that people lived on the other side, people who still hunted and killed whales, in spite of international restrictions. Even in the vast ocean, safety was hard to find.

Without thinking, Callie let her hand slip into the water. It was warmer than she expected; the wavelets caressing her skin tingled pleasantly. Suddenly she sat up straighter and stared at the water around her hand. The tingling sensation sharpened with each passing moment until it felt as if electric sparks were dancing on her palm. She jerked her hand out of the water. The tingling stopped. She examined her hand closely. Slowly, she lowered it again into the water. The prickling sensation instantly resumed, sending shivers of energy up her arm. She gasped and pulled her hand out of the water and stared at the sparks dancing on the surface. She had the strangest feeling that the sea itself was reaching out to her.

She shook her head slowly. "Sorry, Mom, I'm not diving in, if that's what you're after," she muttered, then looked around. She was completely alone as far as the eye could see. "And who, exactly, are you talking to, Callie?" She closed her eyes, as if to reset the program in which she was having a close encounter of the weird kind.

"It's probably just a little sunstroke," she said to herself. "Get a grip." She picked up the paddle and turned the kayak toward the Strait. But before she had gone far, she froze mid-stroke. A cluster of dark shapes bobbed in the water ahead. There looked to be maybe ten or more, floating together. She stared until her eyes watered, afraid to make a move that might scare them off. One of the otters stared back at her. Then it raised a paw and waved at her.

Callie laughed out loud in disbelief. She took one hand off the paddle and waved back. The otters began chuckling and whistling among themselves, slipping under the water and flashing to the surface, blowing bubbles through their whiskers and slapping the water with their paws as they swam toward the kayak.

When they came alongside her, Callie grinned and said, "Hi! I'm so glad to see you."

The otters played for a while in the water beside her before swimming off. Callie tried to relax, but she puzzled over the curious vibration she had felt just before the otters appeared. She lowered her hand again into the water. This time the sensation was even more powerful. Tremors of pleasure and excitement coursed through her veins, and her heart rose on a wave of wordless joy.

Later that day, after she had put away the boat, she reported her discovery to her grandfather, but she didn't tell him about the strange electric sea buzz. She wasn't sure if she'd imagined the whole thing, but she wasn't ready to have her grandfather diminish the mystery with a practical explanation either.

When she returned home, Eel was waiting on the front porch.

"Any luck?" he asked, as she came up and sat next to him.

"Yeah. I know where they are. At least, where some were today." She frowned. "I just hope they'll be there when we go back with him."

Eel nodded. "About that?"

"What?"

"It's gotta be soon. Really soon. And we're gonna have to do it at night. Can we do that?"

"Yeah. I've been thinking the same thing. It will be risky, but if we can get him out of there in the middle of the night—it starts to get light around four a.m.—we should be okay. They probably won't discover he's missing until eight or so. By then, with any luck, we'll already be back." She paused. "We're gonna be in a lot of trouble when they find out."

"Maybe they won't."

Callie sniffed. "I think when they realize he's gone, they're going to figure it out pretty fast."

"They won't have any proof we did it."

"They must have security cameras somewhere. They're bound to guess."

"Guessing doesn't count in court."

She sighed. "I hope you're right."

He pulled her close. Her hair brushed against his cheek.

"You smell like salt water."

She looked up at him. "Yeah. I do. And so will you."

His face was so close she felt the heat of his lips almost upon hers. She pulled back and said quickly, "We can't wait. We've got to do this soon."

Eel raised an eyebrow. "Ready when you are."

She caught the look in his eye and shook her head. "I mean Puki. We've got to get him out of there before they start the big media campaign."

"Too late for that."

"What do you mean?"

"They came today. Television people, photographers. Lights, cameras, action, the whole nine yards. They were there for a couple of hours."

"Why didn't you tell me?"

"Thought you knew. Besides, you were out doing recon. Without me."

She clenched her fists. "This is bad. We'll have to do it tonight."

"All hell's gonna break loose if the kid's not in the tank tomorrow."

"It's not going to get any easier. Once he's famous they'll tighten security."

"'S likely."

She let out a long breath. "Okay. This is it, then. We go tonight."

"What do you want me to do?"

She wrapped her arms around him. He held her and she turned her face up to his. He looked in her eyes and saw green light reflected in them. He kissed her tenderly.

She kissed him back, then pulled away and said, "We don't have time for this now, but hold that thought." She sighed. "Are you as crazy as I am?"

"Guess we'll find out tonight."

"Can you get him out of there by yourself and bring him to the boat?"

"Tell me where it will be and when to be there."

Hunched down in the small skiff at the end of the pier, Callie kept her eyes trained on the parking lot.

"Nice night for a sail."

She jumped. "How did you get here? I was watching for your car."

"Parked on the dark side of the lot. Didn't want to have to explain this if I ran into anyone." He raised the pet carrier with both hands. "He's getting bigger. Maybe twenty pounds?"

Callie peered through the holes in the side of the carrier. Puki's dark eyes shone with reflected light from the marina. "Are you okay, baby?" she whispered.

"He's fine. Seemed like he knew. Jumped into the box by himself."

"Well, that's good. Get in before somebody sees us."

She quickly untied the skiff and switched on the small engine to maneuver out of the boatyard. The sky was free of clouds. Only a sprinkling of distant stars lit the darkness. Once they cleared the inlet, she cut the engine and spread the sail to catch the breeze coming off the Sound.

They didn't talk during the time it took to reach the west coast of Whidbey Island. Callie was afraid to consider the very real possibility that the otters she had seen might be miles away this night.

As they got close to where she had spotted the otters, she dropped the sail and stared into the darkness. What would they do if they couldn't find the otters? They couldn't throw Puki into the water alone. They couldn't hide him someplace. Callie's stomach knotted with anxiety as the minutes passed. She began to wish they'd devised a back-up plan. She glanced at Eel, wondering if he had given any thought to the possibility of failure. He looked perfectly relaxed, gazing out at the sea, as if he stole otters and released them to the wild on a regular basis.

He caught her eye and smiled. "'S nice out here."

"Yeah. It's beautiful." Her foot tapped a restless beat against the bottom of the boat. "I wish we'd find them."

"We've got time," he said.

"Right." Callie hugged herself and tried to relax. No need to panic just yet.

After an hour she felt as if her clothes were too tight and there was sand in her pants. Puki seemed calm, but Callie was ready to jump out of the boat. Wavelets whispered against the hull. The beating of her own heart pounded in her ears.

All of a sudden Eel sat up straighter and said, "Is that them?"

Callie looked where he was pointing, toward a slightly darker patch of water. Straining to see in the darkness, she glimpsed a cluster of small heads bobbing just above the surface.

"Thank God," she breathed.

Puki was on his feet, scrabbling his paws against the sides of the pet carrier.

"D'you think he smells them?" Eel asked.

"Maybe. Probably." Callie gasped at a sharp stab of pain in her chest. What if the others didn't accept him? "Okay. This is it."

She lifted the carrier and looked in at Puki. "Okay, baby. You're gonna be on your own now, okay? But you have to be okay. Okay? Promise me!"

Puki blew air through his whiskers and shook his head.

Callie frowned. "Was that a yes or a no?"

"Come on. It's time. He's got to go now," Eel said.

Callie straightened up. "Can you open the thing? I just... can't."

Eel bent and unhooked the latch. The door swung open, and Puki launched himself into the water. He swam straight to the raft, and as Callie and Eel watched, the otters welcomed him in a flurry of diving, splashing, twirling motion. In the darkness and at a distance, Callie couldn't be one hundred percent sure Puki was accepted, but it looked as though he hadn't been turned away.

Callie and Eel watched until the entire raft swam off together. Then Callie let out the sail. The trip back to Ballard seemed much shorter. They didn't talk.

The sky was light by the time Callie finished tying up the boat. She hugged Eel and whispered, "We did the right thing."

"We did."

She sighed. "I wish we could just go away until all of this blows over."

"You can't run away anymore."

She looked up at him. "What do you mean? I've never run away."

"Well, I have. It only works if nobody wants to find you."

"Who'd want to find me?"

"Me for starters."

"I don't want to run away from you."

"Good." He kissed her.

When she opened her eyes, she looked up at him and said, "Thank you."

"For what?"

"Everything."

"'S best night I've had in a while."

"No. I mean everything. Not just for tonight. For... being... you know."

Eel looked at her quizzically. She stood on her tiptoes and kissed him again.

"I better go. I'm supposed to be at the bakery in an hour."

Eel looked back at the Sound before he turned to her and said, "Guess I'll go face the music then."

"You're practicing in the morning?"

Eel looked back at the boat. "Nah. Going to work." He paused. "Should be interesting."

"Do you want me to come?"

"No." He shifted his weight and said more quietly, "It's gonna get ugly."

"Right. We knew that."

"Right. I didn't tell you that today another TV crew's coming to film a bit on the kid, and when they find him gone, nobody's gonna be happy." He paused. "And when they ask me if I saw anything, I'm gonna tell them I let him go. Just me. You weren't there."

Callie staggered as if she'd been kicked in the chest. "You're not serious!"

"Never been more."

"That's crazy! All you have to do is say you don't know anything. They can't prove anything."

He grabbed her by the arms and lowered his voice. "Callie. They've got cameras. They'll find fingerprints. There's no point in wasting money and time makin' a game of it. I took the kid, and I'm not sorry. I'm proud of what we did tonight. Let me take this one. It won't do any good for us both to be in jail. If I go, the news people will get their story. Maybe it'll help the otters."

"But... you shouldn't go to jail for it."

"I been to jail before. It's not so bad. Not keen on prison. We'll see what happens."

"So were you planning to do this all along?"

"Don't worry about me. I'm skinny, but I'm not weak."

"You should have told me."

"Why? Would we have done something different? There's a price for everything, Callie. Let me pick up the tab this time. 'S only fair."

Callie frowned and kicked a pebble. Seagulls squawked above the marina.

At last she said, "Am I supposed to pretend I had nothing to do with it?"

"For now. Let's see how it plays out."

She shook her head. "I see. So if you're determined to be the hero—"

"Or the villain."

"Or the villain, I can't stop you." She threw her arms around him one last time, and held him close. Then she let go and watched him walk away.

CHAPTER THIRTEEN

When the second batch of muffins slid onto the floor, Celeste said, "Hey. It was funny the first time. Are you sick or something?"

Callie started picking up the ruined muffins and tossing them into the trash. "Sorry, Cele. I didn't get much sleep last night."

Celeste knelt beside her and helped clean up the mess. "Yeah, I noticed you never came home. Where were you?"

"I'd rather not say."

"Why not?"

Callie stood up and wiped her hands on her apron. "I don't want to complicate things any more than they already are."

"Oh really?" Celeste shook her head. "Well, sorry, my dear, but I've got a trashcan full of ruined muffins, and I think I deserve to know why. We don't have secrets, remember?"

Callie sighed. "Yeah. I know. But this is different. If the cops come, I don't want you to have to lie. If you don't know anything, you won't have to."

"Cops? Does this have something to do with the demon lover?"

"He's not my lover!"

Celeste shook her head. "Where did I go wrong? You were out all night, apparently up to no good, and he's still not your lover?"

"I told you... it's complicated."

Celeste gave her a quiet look. "Well, if that's all you can say, I guess maybe you'd better go home for the day. We can't afford to keep throwing food in the trash."

"I'm sorry. I'll make it up to you."

Celeste retrieved a smashed muffin that had rolled under the table. She tossed it in the trash can and said, "I know. If there's anything I can do..."

"Thanks. I'll let you know."

Eel arrived at The Sounding an hour before opening time, and saw a crowd of administrators and staff huddled next to the otter tank. His nerves tightened, but he didn't hang back waiting to be summoned. As soon as they saw him, their questions stormed the air.

"Eel, do you know anything about this?"

"Where's Puki?"

"How could he have gotten out?"

Eel held up his hand for silence. "He's gone."

"Gone! But where? How? How do you know?"

Eel held up his hand again. "I took him away last night. Let him go back to the sea."

A torrent of outraged rebuke erupted from the group.

"What!"

"Are you insane?"

"He'll never survive alone out there!"

Eel stood mute while the furor rose around him. When a window of silence cracked open, Ms. Anderson looked at him gravely and said, "Eel, I can't imagine what you were thinking! There will be consequences for this. We have a responsibility to our patrons and our sponsors, to say nothing of the environmental community. What you've done jeopardizes our whole existence. I'm sorry, but I'm going to have to call the police."

Eel nodded. "'S fine."

One of the marine biologists came up to him and said, "Do you have any idea what you've done? That otter has almost no chance of survival in the wild, alone and not full grown." He turned to the handful of administrators behind him. "This is what happens when you hire unqualified people and don't monitor them. You're lucky he didn't steal all the computer equipment while he was at it."

Eel glowered at him. "Hey! Lighten up. I'm not a thief."

The biologist shook his head, staring at Eel with a look of pained disbelief.

Eel shrugged and recognized a familiar appetite yawning in his chest. For the first time in days he wished he could have a cigarette. Even Callie would understand, he was sure. But he didn't have one, and he doubted he could bum one off any of this crowd. He gazed at the remaining otters in the tank while he waited for the police. Listening to the angry debate echoing over the water, as the administrators and biologists and volunteers argued about how to handle the situation, Eel found himself warming to the idea of a quiet cell.

A few hours later he leaned against the concrete block wall and eyed the man snoring on the lower bunk, who hadn't woken up since Eel had been ushered into the cell. Aside from the snoring, Eel was in no hurry to make his acquaintance. In spite of his blithe comments to Callie, Eel hoped to avoid a long stay in jail. He missed his guitar already. Judging by the resonance of the snoring, the acoustics would be great. Eel felt wired with inspiration after spending the night with Callie on the open sea. When he thought of the way she looked in the boat, with starlight shimmering in her hair, the way her voice floated over the murmur of the waves, the touch of her hand when they released the kid—

He swallowed hard and dug his hands into his pockets and banged his head gently against the bars.

Callie was asleep on the couch, the textbook she had been attempting to read having slipped to the floor, when a hammering noise woke her. She sat up groggily, wondering why no one else was answering the door. Then she remembered it was a work day, and she was home alone, and the reason why hit her like a cold shower. Wide awake, she got up and walked to the door, slowing as she saw Haven's silhouette through the sheers.

His fist was raised to hit the door again when she opened it.

He frowned at her and seemed to inflate for a moment before he spoke.

"Did you have anything to do with this?" he began, leaning inside the threshold.

Callie stepped back. "You want to come in?"

"Answer me! I just had a call from the aquarium. Our otter has been stolen! And I want to know right now if you had anything to do with it."

He loomed over her, his jaw set, his normally bright eyes dark with doubt. Callie felt limp with exhaustion. She was so not in the mood for this. She turned her back on him and walked toward the couch. He followed, bellowing.

"Answer me! Ordinarily I wouldn't believe you could let yourself be a part of some crazy plot, but lately, Callie, I have to say, I've been disappointed by your lack of support."

At this Callie braked hard, her blood pressure shooting up like a bottle rocket. "My what?" She turned and faced him, her hands curled into fists. "My lack of support? I've done nothing but support you since the day we met!"

Haven took a step back. "I know that. I've always admired you for your intelligence and your ability to understand why my work is important. But lately you haven't been as enthusiastic. I thought at first you were sick. But now... tell me—did you know anything about this? Before it happened?"

Callie stared at him sullenly. "What if I did?"

The softness which had crept into Haven's face vanished. "What are you saying?"

"I'm saying, what if I did know something? What if I do know something? So what? I'm not telling you anything."

"Callie! Can you hear yourself? Have you lost your mind? That otter belongs in the aquarium. There's no place better equipped to care for it."

"That otter is a wild animal, and he belongs in the wild!"

Haven gaped at her. "Don't tell me you let him go!"

"I'm not telling you anything."

"Callie—he'll die in the wild. You of all people should know that!"

"No he won't. We made sure he was safe."

A silence collapsed on the room, light as parachute silk, heavy as a mud slide.

"We?"

"Eel helped."

Haven's eyes narrowed. He clenched his teeth and stared at her. "What's happened to you, Callie? You used to be a sensible girl. Now you've jeopardized your career—"

"What career?"

"With me. I can't have my name connected with someone who's seen as a danger to the cause."

"Oh, come on. You think I'm a danger?"

"It doesn't matter what I think. That's how it will appear in the press."

Callie snorted. "Ah. Right. Your press clippings."

"Don't be that way, Callie."

"What way? Honest? You want me just to smile and cheer from the sidelines while you win the day?"

He scowled. "Don't be a bitch."

She recoiled for an instant, then straightened up and said, "You know? Maybe I am a bitch. Maybe it's a good thing you found out. Maybe you'd be better off with someone more refined."

He grabbed her hand and the look in his eye changed. "Callie. Don't do this. I love you. You know that. I just don't understand what's come over you."

"Nothing's come over me! Maybe something's come off of me! You liked me better when I was your little echo, your little cheerleader."

Another silence fell between them, and Callie stood on the edge of it knowing that one more word would send them into the breach of no return. She felt a giddy urge to leap.

"Is this about that guy?" The sudden chill in Haven's voice hit her like a cold slap. "Ms. Anderson told me about your friend the janitor. The one who played guitar for the otters. The one who's in jail now."

Callie took a breath. "It's not about him."

"Are you sure? What's happened to you, Callie? I can't believe you'd have anything to do with someone like that."

She shrugged. "People change."

"I don't."

"Maybe that's your problem."

Haven stiffened. "I don't have a problem. Except that my girlfriend is being used by some con man."

"How can you say that? You don't even know him!"

"I know the type. The 'cool' guy. Honestly Callie, I thought you were too smart for that."

"Huh. Well, I guess I'm not smart enough for you. Why don't you find yourself a girlfriend with a PhD in marketing? You'd be a perfect pair!"

She stormed out of the room, while Haven called after her, "Callie! Come back here! Callie? I forgive you!"

A door slammed at the back of the house, and silence spread like an oil slick on troubled waters.

Callie waited behind the garage until she was sure Haven had left before she went back into the house. She longed to talk with Eel, but she didn't know where he was. If he were in jail, would she be allowed to see him? He would get one phone call, wouldn't he? But would he call her? Did he know her number? Wouldn't it make more sense to call a lawyer? But he wouldn't know any lawyers.

She slumped back onto the couch, her head spinning with anxiety. And running below the main current was a swift channel of worry about Puki. The confident swagger she had put on for Haven was a sham, and she knew it. The truth was, she wished there were some way she could check up on the baby, to verify that he was safe, but she didn't want to leave the house, in case Eel called.

She punched a cushion in frustration. There was nothing to do now but wait.

After an hour of fruitless speculation, Callie turned on the TV to see if the otter story had made the news cycle yet. She nearly choked when the picture shifted almost immediately to an extreme close-up of Puki. He was clutching a clam shell in his paws, and looked as if he was smiling, his button eyes bright. The announcer said his disappearance was under investigation, and police hadn't ruled out kidnapping, or, she added with a journalistic twinkle in her eye, in this case, 'otter napping'.

Callie groaned and switched off the set as the news moved on to other topics. She paced around the room, trying to think how to help Eel avoid getting convicted of anything serious. As she forced herself to consider the ramifications of his being arrested, she realized that the most pressing need would be money to pay for his defense.

By the time Celeste and Viola arrived home Callie was hunched over the dining room table surrounded by piles of scribbled plans and calculations.

"Hey, what's up? That doesn't look like school work," said Celeste.

Callie looked up with bloodshot eyes. "I think we have to raise at least five thousand dollars. Maybe more."

Celeste picked up one of the sheets of paper, skimmed it, and tossed it back on the pile. "Okay. And we need to do this because?"

"Eel's in jail."

"The demon lover?" asked Viola, coming up beside Celeste.

Callie threw her hands in the air. "Would you stop calling him that? Maybe someday. Right now, he's the only suspect in the otter theft, and he has no money and—"

"Whoa, whoa. Back up there, Nellie," said Celeste. "The what? Who stole what?"

"I thought you would have heard about it by now. It's been on all the news stations. It'll be in the paper tomorrow."

"Well, you know how it is when you have your head in the kitchen all day. You miss out on all the good gossip. Someone stole an otter?"

"Not just an otter. My otter. My baby."

Celeste studied Callie for a moment. "Huh. And yet, you're sitting here planning how to raise money to defend the guy who did it?"

"He didn't do it. I mean," she lowered her voice, "okay, you have to swear not to talk about this to anyone. Can you do that?"

Viola shrugged. "I doubt it, Callie. You know us. We talk. If you've got a secret, you'd best be keeping it."

"Fine. Well, then, you'll just have to trust me when I say that Eel is innocent. Better than innocent. And if they put you on the witness stand you can tell them I said so."

Celeste and Viola exchanged a glance.

"So you think it's going to come to that? The witness stand, a jury of his peers, et cetera?"

Callie hung her head. "I don't know what's going to happen. I haven't heard from him since we said goodbye this morning. I thought he might call. You know? How they give them one phone call?"

Her sisters exchanged another glance and sat down at the table across from Callie. Celeste reached out and patted her hand.

"Callie? It sounds to me like this secret of yours might be a little too big for one girl to carry around. So, tell you what. We'll help. And if we get asked questions, we'll take the Fifth."

"I've always wanted to do that," Viola grinned.

"You'd do that for me?"

"Hey. You know us. We're rooting for the demon lover. We want to see you dump Haven and live a little," said Celeste.

Callie smiled a bit sheepishly and said, "Well, in that case I guess you'll be glad to learn that, after last night, I think I'm on the road to hell."

"Yeehah!" Celeste said. "Tell us all about it!"

The phone call finally came at ten o'clock. Callie's end of the conversation was too quiet for her sisters to pick up anything, but her body language spoke volumes. She slumped to the floor gripping the receiver. After five minutes, she hung up.

"Well?" asked Viola.

"I've got some bad news, and some worse news."

"What's the bad news?"

"The bad news is he has to stay in jail at least until after the preliminary hearing."

"And the worse news?"

"If he gets convicted, he could get sent to prison for five years or be fined as much as a hundred thousand dollars. Or both."

"Yikes," said Celeste.

"And they've set bail at fifty thousand." She frowned at the floor and mumbled, "Apparently he's a high flight risk."

Viola nodded. "I guess I can see their point."

"Whoa. That seems a little harsh, considering nobody was hurt by this so-called crime," said Celeste.

"He says the aquarium is arguing that this whole thing is going to—has already—damaged their credibility as trusted stewards of the conservation movement. They claim they're going to lose sponsorship and public support and big bucks as a result, and that it's all Eel's fault." Callie took a breath. "And it's not all his fault. I should be in there with him."

"Don't be a dope! You wouldn't be able to help him at all if you were locked up too. It's your job to show the court that what he did was in the best interests of the animal. And I know you can do it."

Callie sniffed. "I wish I did." She walked over to the table covered with scribbled notes. She grabbed a handful and tossed it up in the air. "I mean, who am I kidding? No matter how much I believe we did the right thing, I don't know how I can convince a judge that we don't deserve to be punished. I never wanted to hurt The Sounding. I love that place." She sat down at the table and put her head in her hands. "I don't know how to fix this."

Viola came over and put her arm around Callie's shoulders. "Hey," she said softly. "We can do this. Together. You, me and Cele. You did a good thing. All we have to do is find a way to show the world."

Callie looked at her. "Five years," she whispered.

Viola tightened her grip. "Hey. You never know. He could get time off for good behavior."

Celeste chuckled. "Oh, not if he's the boy I think he is."

Callie grimaced. "Would you just can it for now?"

"A girl can dream can't she?"

"Not about my boyfriend."

"Fair enough.

CHAPTER FOURTEEN

Eel's court date was set for the last week of June. Callie chafed at the delay, but her sisters claimed it was normal, and that they could use the time to raise money for his defense.

"What defense? He already confessed," she said, as she watered the overgrown collection of rubber plants and palms left by Grandma Linden, who had no space for them in her new home. The plants lent a jungle atmosphere to the sunroom off the kitchen. Viola sat in the wicker rocker petting Cyrano, the enormous orange tabby who also came with the house.

"It's not about whether he confessed," said Viola. "We need to find experts who'll testify that he did the right thing. The prosecution'll be saying that letting Puki go was a bad thing. We have to show that it wasn't."

"I wish I was sure," Callie muttered.

"What?"

"I wish I knew for sure that he's all right. I wish there were some way to prove he's doing fine."

"Do you think you could find him again? Out in the water?"

"It's possible. In theory. I don't know. Why?"

"If you could go out and get some video footage, maybe you could show it in court."

"Forget court. We could put it on YouTube," said Celeste, coming into the room. "The people's court. If we could get a kind of viral support system going—that kind of publicity could turn this thing around."

"Hmm. Maybe." Callie put down the watering can and started pacing. "We could give The Sounding props for doing such a great job raising the baby that he could make the transition back to the wild. That'd be good for them. If I can get footage..." She stopped pacing. "It's a big if."

"True. But you have the gift, Callie. The magic water thingy. If anyone can find that otter again, it's you." Celeste smiled at her. "Gosh, you know? This could be really exciting. We should write a song for Puki, like Eel did."

"And we could have a benefit concert," said Viola.

Callie nodded. "Okay. Okay. One thing at a time. You write a song. I'm gonna go find a camera." She skipped out of the room.

"Cool. We have a plan. A strategy. I feel so empowered," said Celeste, flexing her biceps.

"You were born empowered," said Viola.

"Yes, well. I've been holding back. It'll be nice to let 'er rip."

"Okay Wonder Woman, to the piano."

Later that evening, the sisters watched the six o'clock news to see if the otter story was still making headlines. Callie curled up on the couch and stared at the screen, hoping the news people had better things to do with their time than dwell on The Sounding.

The top stories covered a shooting in Capitol Hill and a sink hole near the University Bridge. Then an image of Puki's smiling face appeared with the headline, "Otter Plotter?" The reporter recounted the basic facts, adding the latest news that Eel's court date had been set. When a mug shot of Eel came on the screen, Celeste said, "Oh, they cut his hair!"

"No. He did," said Callie.

"I liked it long," said Viola.

"At least it's still green," said Celeste.

"Hush," Callie said. "I want to hear this."

The reporter's voice grew more strident as she launched into a different segment of the story, with sound bites from aquarium officials and critics. Callie listened calmly to Ms. Anderson talking about how hard The Sounding works to safeguard the creatures in its care, but when Haven's square jaw and stern gaze filled the screen she flinched and said, "Oh my God. What's he doing there?"

The reporter introduced Haven as a local environmental activist who specializes in water habitats. Haven immediately launched into a brisk critique of policies which failed to protect sensitive natural areas. "Sadly, this incident is further proof that we can't save our natural resources by constructing artificial enclaves in which to imprison them. Wild creatures belong in the wild, and unless we can preserve our wilderness areas, the creatures whose existence depends on them will be forced into gulags such as The Sounding, where lack of vital resources can prove deadly to the very creatures we hope to protect."

"Wow," said Celeste. "He's never at a loss for words, is he?"

Callie hit the mute button. "So was he coming down on our side? Was I hearing him right?"

Viola shrugged. "Well, he did say that bit about 'wild creatures belong in the wild'."

"That was really strange." Callie uncurled her legs and wriggled her toes, which had gone tingly.

"Hearing Boyfriend Number One weighing in on Boyfriend Number Two's case?" asked Celeste.

"Yeah." Callie massaged her calves. "I wonder if he's going to show up at the trial."

"You gotta be ready for anything, Callie. But don't worry. Once you get that video, the world will see that Puki's better off free."

Callie walked to the window and stared out at the street, where a couple of neighborhood kids were shooting hoops. In the quiet room, the bouncing ball sounded like an arrhythmic heartbeat. Callie tapped her foot in time before asking, "Did you guys come up with a song?"

"Not yet. We've got a couple of ideas, but we're thinking the song needs to be radio friendly. Punchier than our usual stuff, with a catchy refrain and a strong beat." Viola paused before she added, "We need a back-up band."

Callie nodded. "Maybe I should talk to Squid."

"Who?"

"He's in Eel's band."

"Eel has a band? I'm loving him more and more," said Celeste.

"It's not much of a band. Mainly him and Squid. He plays keyboards. And they might have a drummer and a bass player."

"Well what are you waiting for?"

"I thought you said the song wasn't ready."

"It's not. But five heads are better than two. Or whatever. They're bound to want to help Eel too. We should get together and work out the song with them."

"Or songs."

"Right. For the benefit concert."

Callie turned away from the window. "I wish we could get Eel out so he could play. He and Squid have worked up a lot of songs already."

"How much is his bail?"

"Fifty thousand."

"Hmm. So, we really only need to come up with like five thousand to get him out. We've got that much in savings."

"But you need to put up some collateral," said Viola. "We don't have anything worth fifty thousand."

Celeste looked at her. "Except the bakery."

Viola shook her head. "We can't do that Cele. It's not ours."

"I think Grandpa would take a chance on Eel if Callie asks him."

In a silence broken only by the staccato of bouncing basketballs outside, Callie turned and stared out the window while an imaginary shot clock counted down. "I'll do it."

Viola walked over and put her hand on Callie's shoulder. "Do you really think you can trust Eel?"

"I do."

"I hope you're right."

Grandpa Linden poured a cup of coffee and spooned some sugar into it before he spoke.

"How did you meet this boy?"

"He's not a boy. He's a man."

Grandpa took a sip of coffee. "All right. How did you meet this young man?"

"I pulled him out of the lake."

Grandpa gazed at her curiously. "What was he doing in the lake?"

"I don't know. He fell in."

"And you fished him out."

"Yes."

"Hmm." He stirred his coffee. "Well, it could signify. Could be a coincidence, but I suspect the other thing."

"What do you mean?"

"You pulled this fella out of the water, Callie. Doesn't that tell you anything?"

"I don't know. I've pulled other guys out of the lake."

"But this one is different?" He paused, studying her face. "I'm asking you."

Callie hesitated, tracing patterns in the spilled sugar on the table. "He is different. And it's not just me. Puki—the otter—he likes Eel. Eel plays music for him. Or he did, before all this happened."

Grandpa nodded, his eyes flickering with amusement. "Doesn't sound like he belongs in jail then."

"Then you'll help?"

"I've always liked eels."

Callie smiled. "Thanks Grandpa. We won't let you down."

"There's no way you could."

Two days of paperwork later, Eel walked out of jail and into Callie's arms.

She was waiting for him just outside the door, and practically threw herself against him. After several breathless fierce kisses, he pulled away and looked into her eyes.

She stared back, as if daring him to say anything. He smiled and whispered in her ear, "I guess it was worth it."

She looked up at him. "What?"

"Going to jail. If this is my reward."

She punched his chest. "It's not funny. I'm not going to wait for you if they lock you up for five years."

Eel loosened his hold. "I wouldn't ask you to."

"Just so we have that straight."

They started walking.

"Where are we going?" he asked.

"To practice."

"Practice?"

"Band practice. Squid and Bob and Duggan are all waiting at your place. We've got a benefit concert lined up in two weeks. We've got a lot of work to do."

Eel stopped walking and stared at her.

"Your friend Tommy and his girlfriend, they're helping. My sisters are writing some songs too. We're going to perform together."

Eel shook his head. "I should go to jail more often."

She hit him again. "Don't say that!"

He bowed to her.

"Cut that out."

"As you wish," he said, bowing again.

She fought a smile. "Are you trying to make me mad?"

"Punish me. Please."

"Oh shut up," she laughed, and ran ahead to the car.

During the next week Callie and Eel spent every free moment together. They worked on songs with the new band, practiced performing with her sisters, went out searching for Puki, and met with a lawyer to discuss defense strategies.

Dwight Chubb, an attorney who offered his services at a reduced rate because his girlfriend was a member of PETA, was a tall slender man in his mid-thirties with shiny pink cheeks and thinning red hair. But it was the fiery gleam in his eyes that gave Eel hope.

The first thing he said to them after they sat down in his office was, "I believe you did the right thing. The problem is, the law isn't always about what's right. The Sounding can make a strong case that you relinquished ownership when you brought the otter in."

"But if they were a pet boarding place—" Callie began.

"But they're not," Chubb interrupted. "I'll be arguing that you never meant for the otter to stay permanently at The Sounding... whether or not that's the case." He looked from Callie to Eel. "We can hope that the judge will be lenient because of your youth and because there was no intent to harm the animal, or The Sounding. But you should be prepared for the worst."

"You mean jail?" Callie asked.

"Possibly. Possibly a stiff fine."

"How stiff?" Eel asked.

"There's no way to know. It could be ten thousand dollars. Or more. If the judge is hard-nosed."

"Won't we have a jury?" Callie asked.

"Not in this sort of case." Chubb tapped his pen on the desk for a few seconds before continuing. "Judges are only human, you know. They base their decisions on a lot of factors... the law, of course, but they've got opinions of their own... personalities..." He paused and looked at Eel. "Can you do something about your hair?"

"Like what?" asked Eel.

"Does it have to be green?"

"Does yours have to be red?"

Callie interrupted. "It shouldn't matter. The color of his hair. What kind of judge would even think about that?"

"Judges are human. They have likes and dislikes, prejudices. Just like the rest of us. You don't want to give the judge any extra reason to dislike you. That's why I advise you to dress nicely and control your emotions in the courtroom."

Eel shook his head. "This is the color my hair is. I'm not dying it black for the judge."

"I'm not suggesting that. Can't you wash it out?"

"I haven't dyed it in months. It keeps comin' in like this. Nothin' I can do about it, okay?"

Chubb shrugged. "Okay. I don't know anything about hair dye."

"Maybe you should dye your hair green. For the court date. You know, for solidarity," Callie said.

Chubb put down his pen and said, "I guess we're done here for now. I take it you haven't had any luck getting a video of the otter in the wild?"

"No. We've been trying, but—"

"'S lot of water out there. He's a little guy," said Eel.

Chubb nodded. "I'm not sure it would help anyway. But it would be nice to be able to show the judge that the animal is alive and well."

"But how would they know it was him anyway?" asked Callie. "I mean, we could get footage of any otter and say it was him."

"We're not doing that," said Eel.

"I know but—"

"It's better to have nothing at all than to present false evidence," said Chubb. "Then you'd really be in trouble."

"Like we're not now?" said Callie.

Chubb shrugged. "What you did was... well, misguided at the very least. It's possible a judge might be persuaded to see it as somehow noble, in a "Free Willy" sort of way. But if the judge starts to doubt your sincerity or your integrity, things won't go well."

CHAPTER FIFTEEN

Callie and Eel kept searching, but they saw no otters. Eel kept his doubts to himself. He could see the tension in Callie's face and hear the sorrow in her voice, and he felt responsible for encouraging her to let the baby go. As the days went by, the effort to maintain a positive front for her sake wore him down.

One night on the ride back to his apartment, the fatigue that he'd been ignoring for days settled on him like a lead shirt. He stumbled getting out of the car and tramped across the grass to the building entrance. At the sound of laughter from above, he glanced up to his apartment. The window was open, a square of light in the darkness.

He had no idea what time it was, but it felt late. Stepping inside the apartment, he stopped and blinked at the surprise visitors. Squid and Tommy and Abby were sitting on the floor. Seated next to them were a tanned attractive woman with a small child in her arms, and a lean, olive-skinned, rugged man with greenish black hair.

The weight of the day slipped from Eel's shoulders. "Green Man!" he said, stepping forward with an outstretched hand. Fergus rose and held his arms open. The handshake became a hug. When they separated, Eel said, "Didn't expect to see you. Nor you, Alice," he added with a slight bow.

Fergus glanced at Tommy. "Tom called and told us about your trouble. He thought we might be able to help."

Tommy stood up and said, "I asked Mom to bring Fergus here. We think he would be a good character witness for the trial."

"Do I need one of those?"

"Well. You are a character," said Alice.

Eel grinned. "It's nice to see you, too. The kid's grown."

Alice smiled. "Her eyes are turning greener too."

Eel caught Fergus staring at him.

"You've changed," Fergus said.

Eel shrugged. "Everybody changes. Cut the hair."

"It's not just the hair."

Abby interjected, "I like that you're keeping it green."

Eel shrugged again. "Yeah. Don't know about that. Guess the chemicals sunk into my skull." He scratched his head.

Fergus continued to stare.

"Eel, Tommy's been telling us about this magic otter you found," said Alice.

"I didn't find him. Callie did."

"She's your girlfriend?"

"Something like that." He glanced at Fergus and noticed a warmer light in the older man's eyes. "Listen, I'd like to talk, but, it's been a long day and—"

"And we have a gig tonight," said Squid.

Eel gaped at him.

"You forgot?" Squid asked.

Eel shook his head in a dazed way. "Can't believe I forgot about it."

"Yeah, well. You can grab some dinner at the club. We need to go now."

Eel looked at Alice and said, "I'm sorry I can't talk."

"It's okay," she said. "I need to get the baby to bed anyway. Fergus can go to your gig, so you'll get a chance to talk with him."

"Great. I hope I'll get to talk to you too. Might be goin' to jail though."

"We heard," Alice said. "That's why we came. You were there for us when we were in trouble. Now we're here for you."

Eel managed a smile. The baby nestled on Alice's shoulder stared into his eyes. He raised his hand to the baby and the little girl wrapped her tiny fingers around one of Eel's. His grin widened. "She's strong."

"Like her mother," said Fergus, coming closer.

"I'm glad you guys came," Eel said.

"I'm coming back to hear you play," Fergus said as he went out the door.

After the group left Squid asked, "What's up with that guy? You called him Green Man?"

"'S long story. He... you wouldn't believe it."

"Try me."

Eel put his hands up in a 'don't ask me' gesture and said, "He's from another world. The Green Men take care of all the plants and stuff. They got some kind of green magic. Fergus came here through a door in a tree. It was his special tree, like his hook-up to the magic? Alice's ex-husband, Tom's dad, cut down the tree. Now Fergus is stuck here—mortal, like the rest of us."

Squid stared at Eel for a minute. Then he nodded his head slightly and said, "Thought he seemed different."

Sometime after the third set Eel stepped out into the alley behind the club to grab a smoke. In the uncertain future he saw before him, the no-smoking idea seemed like a waste of effort.

Another shadow fell across the alley. Fergus was silhouetted by the streetlamp. "I like your band," he said.

"Thanks."

"Tom tells me you played for the otter."

"Yeah. He liked it." Eel nearly smiled. "That's how all the trouble started, I guess."

Fergus leaned against the wall. "Had that ever happened before?"

"What d'you mean?"

"Did an animal ever respond to your music before?"

Eel raised an eyebrow. "Depends on your definition of an animal I s'pose."

Fergus remained silent.

Eel continued, "Nothing like that ever happened before. The way he lit up. He... I knew he was really hearing me—you know?" He took a drag off his cigarette. "Sounds crazy. But if you saw him—"

"How old are you now?"

"Twenty-one. How old are you?"

"No one counts years in the Realm. Everyone simply exists. Forever."

"But you're here now."

"Yes."

"So you're gonna grow old like the rest of us."

"Yes."

"Must be a drag, after bein' immortal and all."

"I have no regrets. I'm happy. Happier than I've ever been."

"Lucky you."

Fergus gave him a look. "You could be lucky too."

"You think so? I might be going to jail. Got no job. No future." He turned with a half grin toward Fergus. "Lucky me."

Fergus said, "Let me buy you a drink."

"Won't say no to that."

Back inside the bar, the noise and crowd made conversation difficult, except for the most drunken kind, and Fergus didn't seem inclined in that direction this night. But as they sipped their drinks, the Green Man leaned close enough to ask in an undertone, "How well did you know your father?"

Eel eyed him curiously. "It's been a long time since anyone asked me about him. I never knew him. My mom never talked about him much. She was a hippie... lived in a commune, somewhere in

California. Dancin' naked on the beach, free love, the whole bit. Then she met my dad, and he kind of spoiled it. That's how I came along. And he disappeared. Before I was born, I'm told. I don't know anything about him except that my mom was never happy as long as I knew her."

"Where is she now?"

"She died when I was thirteen. Car accident. I stayed with my gran a couple of years. That's how I wound up in Virginia. Been on my own ever since."

Fergus mused silently. "So you don't know much about who you really are then?"

"I guess not."

Squid came up alongside the two men and tilted his head toward the stage. "We should play," he said.

Eel nodded, and raised his glass to finish his drink.

Fergus shifted closer and said, "I'd like to talk more in private later."

Eel gave him a look. "What is there to say?"

Fergus held his gaze. "There might be a thing or two you don't know."

Eel put his empty glass down on the bar with a thunk. "Great. We'll talk later."

He strode back to the stage, strapped on his guitar, and began to play. The rest of the band fell into rhythm with him. Fergus watched and listened with a blend of amusement and affection. He looked at the crowd pressing up against the stage and saw the rapt attention in their faces. Eel stood alone in the glow of a blue spotlight casting deep shadows on the bones of his face.

Back at the apartment, Fergus began by asking, "What made you come up here? To Seattle?"

Eel shrugged. "Dunno. Mitch and Natalie wanted to move here. Said the music scene was good."

"You didn't want to stay with us in California?"

"Too much sunshine. It's not natural."

"So... there was no particular reason you came to this area?"

Eel shook his head. "What's your point?"

"You're not aware of the great forests in the Olympics?"

"They have trees in the Olympics?"

"I'm talking about the Olympic Peninsula, west of here. It holds some of the largest stands of old-growth forest in this part of the world."

Eel nodded. "Okay. That's your thing. Trees."

Fergus looked at him carefully. "Maybe it's your 'thing' too."

Eel snorted. "Me? I'm not into trees, man. I mean—I got nothin' against 'em. But, you know? They're just trees."

The muscles in Fergus's jaw twitched slightly. He shifted in his seat and asked, "How did you meet Callie?"

As Eel explained how Callie had pulled him out of the lake, a trace of a smile crossed Fergus's face. "I want to hear more about your music, and the otters. How did that connection begin?"

"It's just the one. Puki. Callie found him. And then I met him. And he... he likes me."

"Maybe the otter can tell that Callie likes you," said Squid, sitting down beside him.

"Maybe."

"Hey dude, she's crazy about you. Anyone can see it."

"I don't know. I think if it came to a choice between me and the otter she'd take the otter."

"You're nuts, man."

"That's what they all say." Eel eyed Fergus, who had been studying him during this exchange. "What do you say, Green Man?"

Fergus leaned forward with his elbows on his knees and his hands clasped in front of him. "Here's what I think. You never knew your father. You've never been sick a day in your life—"

"How'd you know that?" Eel interrupted.

Fergus continued smoothly, "You've got a way with music that goes beyond the ordinary. You have more power than you know. You're devilishly handsome, and your hair... well," he pulled at his own straggling greenish locks. "It's a look not everyone can pull off."

Eel stared at him. "What are you saying?"

The whine of a distant siren broke the silence, but no one spoke until Squid said, "Okay. Maybe everyone else got the Cliff notes on this, but for those of us who missed the assignment, what are you driving at?"

Fergus smiled. "I'd like Eel to figure it out himself. He's a smart boy."

Eel stared at him as the seconds ticked by.

"So, what? You're my Dad?"

Fergus chuckled. "No. Though I'd be proud to make the claim, it's not possible. I never came through to this world in the last fifty or so years before I came to Alice. But I know Green Men who did. And California in the eighties? A popular spot to make merry."

"So you think I'm half-green man?"

"I think it's possible. I doubt you're an ordinary human."

Eel sat back, as if exhaustion had caught up with him at last. "Maybe I can use that in court. Not guilty, your honor, on account of not being human."

Squid laughed. "This explains a lot."

The smile faded from Fergus's face as he watched Eel sinking into himself. The younger man stared at the floor without speaking before he looked up and said, "Why should I believe you?"

"Because you know it's true. It's in your bones. In your blood. You're not like other humans."

Eel shook his head. "Even if that's true, it doesn't mean I'm some kind of green freak. I'm just a guy who plays music. I'm nothing special."

"You don't believe that."

Eel rolled his eyes. "You know what's funny? If you'd told me a year ago, a few months ago even, that I was something special, some kind of superman, I'd have bought it. No question. But now? 'S funny. I know what special is now. And I'm not it. I'm just a guy with a guitar. And a bad haircut. There's a million guys like me."

Fergus shook his head. "There are none like you. Green Men are scarce in this world, I can tell you. But the hybrid children of Green Men and mortals are rarer than phoenix feathers, more precious than mermaid's scales."

"Yeah, about those? Not as rare as you might think."

Fergus narrowed his eyes. "What do you mean?"

"Callie. If you put together the evidence and figured out I'm some kind of green half-breed, maybe you can figure out Callie's seagirl vibe. She's half-mermaid. Or something like it."

"Did she tell you this?"

"Her mother told her. Her mom claimed that she was a mermaid before she ran off. She told Callie she had 'the gift,' whatever that is." He frowned. "I didn't believe it at first, but... if you heard her sing... if you saw her on the water..." He shrugged. "I don't know. I don't know what's real anymore."

"Interesting," said Fergus.

Eel eyed him soberly. "I guess it doesn't matter anyway."

Squid interrupted. "Man, what's wrong with you?"

"Once I'm in jail, she'll go back with her old boyfriend, the save-the-planet guy. That's what she loves. It's the mission. That's what matters to her."

Squid sat down on the edge of the couch and said, "Listen man, I don't know much about women, or the mission, or whatever, but I know love when I see it, and that woman loves you. I'd bet my life on it."

"So what? Even if she does, I'm not the guy for her. I'm not Mr. Savin' the World Guy. I'm not gonna save the whales and the dolphins and shit. Hell, I can't even swim. She loves that guy because he fights the good fight. And, you know what? She should love him. Because he's the kind of guy she deserves. She'd be better off without me."

Fergus listened quietly until Eel finished. Then he turned to Squid and said, "I think he needs a nap."

Eel gaped at him for a split second before punching his shoulder. "I'll nap you."

Fergus smiled. "All right. We can talk more tomorrow. I'm leaving. But don't make plans for next week. You and I have work to do."

"What? I don't have time for games. Gotta get a job. Pay my debt to society."

"We'll get started on that too. But you need to understand who you really are."

Eel looked at Squid and shook his head. "Tell me all about it tomorrow. I'm going to sleep." He went into the bedroom and closed the door.

Squid lowered his voice and said, "You really think that's true? What you told him? About his dad?"

"I've suspected something of the sort since I met him. His aura is a different hue from other humans. Back in Virginia I thought it might be a result of taking drugs. But here his aura has grown stronger, as if he's drawing power from some other source."

"Could that happen?"

"It's hard to say. It could be simply a reflection of the fact that he's in love. Or it could be because he's physically close to the portal through which his father came."

Squid considered this. "And... that would be a tree?"

"Yes."

Squid nodded. He stretched out on the couch and said, "Cool." He stared up at the ceiling. "They got a lot of trees around here."

CHAPTER SIXTEEN

"Close your eyes," Fergus said.

Eel rolled them first, then obeyed. He shifted the backpack on his shoulders. "What now?"

"Just listen. Don't think. Listen."

Eel took a deep breath. The air was heavy with the scent of pine, underlaid with ferns and damp earth. A Stellar's jay squawked in the canopy above. As the seconds slid by, Eel began to hear more sounds—the tiny snik of a bird tapping on tree bark, the rustle of leaves, a wet whisper from a distant stream.

"How long do I have to do this?"

"Give it time. You can hear better with your eyes closed."

"What am I listening for?"

"I can't tell you that. You'll know when you hear it."

"Is this some Carlos Casteneda trick?" asked Squid, sitting on a fallen trunk.

"Who?" asked Fergus.

"The guy in the books about the mysteries of the desert and stuff."

"I'm not familiar with them. We're here to see if Eel can find a clue to his own mystery."

"How will he know—"

"Shhhh." Eel held his hand up.

While Fergus and Squid watched, Eel slowly turned around so that he was facing another direction. He took a step forward, still with his eyes closed. Then he took another. Then he tripped over a root and went crashing to the ground.

"Ow," he said, sitting up and rubbing his knees, his eyes open. He looked at Fergus. "What was that?"

"A root."

"No, that sound."

"What did you hear?"

Eel peered into the woods. "Not sure really. Kinda sounded like music, maybe. Pipes? Drums? No guitar. I don't know. It was far away. Maybe I imagined it."

Fergus stared at him. "You didn't imagine it. I can hear it too."

"Hey! I can't hear anything," said Squid. "Except the squirrels."

"No, you wouldn't," Fergus said. "What Eel heard is beyond the perception of ordinary mortals." He turned to Eel. "I hoped that if we came close enough to a portal that you would be able to sense the world beyond. Even though you can never go through, whatever you inherited of your father's power allows you to hear the music of the Realm."

"Wait," Squid interrupted. "You're saying there's portals here? Right here in River City?"

Fergus gave him a blank look.

Squid shrugged. "Sorry. You had to be in marching band. I mean, Eel's dad lives somewhere around here?"

"That I can't say. Eel's father could be anywhere. This forest is far too vast for us to search for one tree. But I hoped that if we came here, Eel would be able to feel the flow of magic that leaks through the portals. It seems I was right."

Eel stood up. "How come you can hear it? I thought you said once your tree was cut down you lost all that Green Man stuff."

"It's true that I lost my 'Green Man stuff' as you call it. That tree alone was my entry into the Timeless Realm. But I can still hear the music that leaks through. Although I can use the knowledge gained from centuries of visiting Earth and nurturing its green world, I can no longer tap into the energy that abides in the Realm. But you... yours is a different destiny. As long as your father's tree lives, you should be able to draw upon that energy, should you choose the Green Path."

"So I could grow a righteous crop of pot?"

"You might be able to do much more than that. Perhaps restore ravaged forests. Or make the desert bloom. You could renew barren fields."

"How? I know you could do that stuff before you gave it all up for Alice. But I don't get how I'm all of a sudden supposed to have some kind of green power just 'cause I can tune in the Radio Free Tree station."

"At this point you have little magical power, nor do you have the skill to use it even if you did. However, now that we know it's here, in this forest, you can begin training."

"What do you mean?"

"Magic is like a muscle which must be exercised to develop its full potential. Up to now, you've never attempted to direct your latent gifts, with the exception of your music. Your obvious talent in that area alone should convince you that you have more ability than the average human."

Squid nodded at Eel and said, "I knew you were too good to be a regular human."

Eel shook his head. "If I'm so special, how come Callie doesn't see it?"

"She does, man! She was ready to go slumming with you when she thought you were a mere mortal. Wait till she learns you've got the green mojo. She's gonna be all over you."

Eel looked at Fergus and saw that the former Green Man wasn't sharing the glee.

"I haven't met Callie," said Fergus, "but while you're developing your skills and learning the limits of your powers, it would be best if you kept this secret." He looked at Squid. "I trust you understand."

"Sure, man. The secret identity. I'm sealed."

Fergus looked at Eel, who said, "Squid doesn't talk. And when he does no one understands him anyway."

"Well, then," said Fergus, "I suggest we try a few experiments, to get some idea of your power."

Eel grimaced. "Does this mean I have to watch grass grow?"

"It might not be as boring as you think," said Fergus.

After several hours spent trying to make ferns bend to his will, Eel dropped to a seat on a damp, fallen tree trunk and said, "I don't know. If this is as good as it gets, it's nowhere near good enough."

Fergus sat beside him. "Don't be discouraged. What you're trying to do is open an eye inside yourself that's been closed all your life. It will take time, even after it's open, for you to understand what it is you're seeing."

Squid raised his eyebrows. "And they tell me I'm hard to understand."

Fergus reached behind the tree trunk and pulled a fern leaf closer, until it was only inches from Eel's face.

"This leaf, which you see as a flat, still, surface of green, is actually full of movement, depth and energy. Ordinary humans can't see the radiant life in plants because they're so absorbed in the surface of their own lives, and they've never been taught to respect the things they can't see with their limited vision. Some of your kind with an interest in science make the effort to improve their understanding, using microscopes and such, but you, with your genetic link to the green world, should be able to see into the plants, without the aid of special devices."

"Why can't I, then?" said Eel, stubbing his boot against the peaty forest floor.

"Maybe you're trying too hard. When a flower blooms, the petals unfurl. When your inner eye opens, it's the same way. As you relax and let it open, more light will enter – like a camera lens – and you will see that the flat green surface of the leaf is not flat at all. Nor is it static. It hums with life. It sparkles with activity."

"Sparkles, eh?" Eel peered at the fern below his chin. "I'll take your word for it. But so what? What good is it if I can see things? Big deal. Any doper on mescaline sees things other people don't, and it doesn't change anything. If this is your idea of magic, it's... well, I mean, come on—I know there's more than that. When you did that light thing for Alice's garden—the big web thing—that was magic. Am I gonna be able to do that?"

"What big web thing?" Squid asked.

"He made this big, like, net of light, green light, that kept anyone from hurting the garden. Was pretty cool."

"I'd like to see that."

"The Web of Protection is a specialized magic that can only be used when there is a compelling threat to some part of the natural world," Fergus said. "It's not a magic trick to be used lightly for entertainment."

"Was pretty entertaining, though," said Eel, looking at Squid. "People came from miles around to see it."

"Sorry I missed it."

"The point is," Fergus said, "we don't really know what sort of magic will respond to you. It could be that you'll be able to summon a force such as the Web, if the need arises. But it will take time for you to learn how to use your skill. Even after you find it."

"Great. Well I've had enough for today." Eel stood up and swatted at the moss clinging to his pants.

Fergus watched him with a slight smile. "All right. But Alice and I will have to go back to Berkeley after the trial. I hope you'll keep working on your skills."

"Sure, for all the good it'll do me."

"Just keep at it. It'll grow on you." Fergus glanced at Eel's pants and smiled. "That's an old Realm joke. Although, trust me, moss is no joke."

"Hah. The joke's on Seattle," said Squid, as they walked out of the forest.

CHAPTER SEVENTEEN

Stressed by daily stories in the press and letters to the editor, Callie was having trouble sleeping. Public reaction was generally negative. Some of the most vitriolic letters came from critics who claimed that the otter incident was evidence that the aquarium was a waste of taxpayer money. And then there were the letters expressing outrage that even wild animals got better treatment than homeless people.

Callie felt she had let everyone down—from Puki to The Sounding to Eel himself, who was unable to relieve the guilt that tormented her.

"You gotta stop thinking this way Callie," he said. "We'll find the kid. We'll make everything right."

Yet his stoic calm, far from reassuring her, only made her feel frustrated at being forced to let him face the legal consequences alone. Every time she tried to discuss it with him they argued. He insisted she keep quiet about her part in Puki's release.

Finally, she slipped away and found Grandpa Linden sitting in the sunshine in his backyard, a pile of newspapers at his feet.

"It's quite a mess you've made of things, eh girl?"

In the soft morning breeze, Callie's blonde curls, wildly tangled from another sleepless night, floated around her face like the tendrils of a sea anemone.

"I don't know what to do," she said. "We can't find him. We've looked all over. And now..." She looked into her grandfather's gray eyes. "I'm really worried."

Grandpa Linden nodded. He kicked at the pile of papers. "You got 'em all stirred up."

"I never meant to. I just wanted to put Puki back where he belonged. Now Eel might go to prison. And it's all my fault. I should be on trial. With him."

Grandpa Linden appeared to study the clouds for a moment. "And why aren't you?"

"He says there's no point in both of us going to jail. I can't let him take all the blame, but if I say anything he's going to be mad."

"I see." He gave the clouds some more of his attention. "Tell me this. You did what you thought was right?"

"Yes."

"Do you still think it was right?"

"Yes."

"Then own it. Be proud of it. No matter what your Eel fella says. If he's worth anything at all, he's got to understand that he can't take this from you. You can be proud of it together."

"Thanks Grandpa," she said, giving him a hug. "Can I use your phone?"

At the sheriff's office, whatever nervousness Callie felt about confessing disappeared within minutes. The first officer she spoke to made no effort to hide his skepticism and seemed to think she was only offering her story out of sympathy for her boyfriend. He suggested she go home and let the system work.

After she got angry and insisted they document her confession, another officer took over and made it clear that he didn't find anything amusing in her story.

"You realize we could lock you up right now? According to your statement, you not only aided the suspect in committing the crime, but you also attempted to cover up your role in it, which adds obstruction of justice to the charges against you." The officer loomed over Callie like a dark blue rain cloud, but she felt lighter than she had in days.

"I understand. That's why I'm here."

The officer glared at the papers in front of him. He looked at Callie and said, "In view of the fact that you came in of your own free will, and you have no prior record, I'm going to let you go for now. You'd better get a lawyer and show up in court, or you'll be in worse trouble than you're in already." He handed her a summons and dismissed her.

Callie's head spun as she walked out into the sunshine. She was exhilarated to be rid of her guilty secret, but in its place was apprehension about Eel's reaction. She had never seen him mad.

She decided to wait until after practice that night to tell him. But with the secret weighing on her mind, she forgot words and missed cues to the point that Viola asked her if she was coming down with something.

When they finally called it a night, Callie declined Viola's offer of a ride home, saying she needed to talk to Eel. Her sisters nudged her jokingly as they left. Callie ignored their innuendos. They'd learn soon enough what she'd done.

He came up behind her and slipped his arms around her waist, kissing her neck softly as he whispered, "I thought they'd never leave."

She took a breath. "I have to tell you something."

"Yeah. We have to 'talk'." He smiled as he said this, turning her gently to face him. The look in her eyes wiped away his smile. "What's wrong?"

"It's... I didn't want you to read about it in the papers."

"I don't read the papers."

"I know, but... I went to the police today. I told them I helped you."

"Why?"

"I can't let you take all the blame! Puki is my problem as much as yours. More. It's not right for you to—"

"What do you mean, 'more'?"

"I mean I found him. I took him to the aquarium in the first place. If I hadn't—"

"If you hadn't he'd be dead already."

"He might be dead already."

"It's not your fault if he is."

"Yes it is! I don't know!" She hung her head. When she looked back at him, her eyes glistened with tears. "I only know I have to do this. You have to let me take my share of the blame."

Without a word Eel pulled her close and held her. She closed her eyes and felt his ribs moving slightly under her cheek. Somewhere in the distance a train whistled. She heard the beat of Eel's heart. Its curious rhythm reminded her of something foreign and enticing, like a tango. She peered into his face as if seeing it for the first time.

The next morning, she worked the early shift, so she had a few hours of mixing, kneading and baking before the first customers showed up for coffee and crullers.

The newspaper vending machines on the sidewalk were filled by then, and Callie scurried out and grabbed a copy, hoping to read it before Celeste arrived. When a quick scan revealed no mention of her confession, she enjoyed a few moments of relief, but Celeste's arrival quickly put an end to it.

"I thought we'd agreed to let him play the hero," said Celeste, pushing through the door to the kitchen.

"Oh, hi," said Callie.

"Well? When did you decide to throw yourself on the pyre? Isn't it enough that we have to worry about keeping your boyfriend out of jail? Now we have to hire a lawyer for you?"

"We're going to share the lawyer."

Celeste put her hands on her hips and eyed Callie sternly. "Oh really? How did he take it when you told him you'd decided to book a room at the Prison Arms?"

"Actually, he was very sweet. We're thinking of writing a song about our life behind bars."

"Have you both gone nuts?"

Callie shrugged and stopped trying not to grin. "I think maybe we have. And it feels so great!"

Celeste relaxed her stance. "I see. Well. I guess that's the way it's going to be. I suppose we can always bake you a torte with a file in it."

"Or file a tort with a cake in it," said Viola, who had come in while they were talking.

Callie wiped her hands on a towel and said, "It might not be so bad. We might not get time."

"Humph," Celeste snorted. "You'll do time around here, missy, paying us back for all the money this is going to cost."

"And I will too. But maybe we'll make a lot at the concert."

"Right. And maybe they'll find an environmentally friendly substitute for oil in our lifetime. Keep dreamin' kid."

Callie went to wait on a batch of customers. When they had cleared out she stuck her head back inside the kitchen and asked, "How did you hear about it? I didn't see anything in the paper."

"Oh, the radio is way ahead of the paper. But don't worry. I'm sure they'll catch up before the day is out."

By lunch time a cluster of reporters and photographers were camped out on the sidewalk, waiting for Callie to get off work. Celeste had shooed them all out of the bakery earlier. "Either buy a pastry or clear out," she'd told them.

Peeking at them from behind the half-curtains, Callie said, "Do you think I could sneak out the back?"

"No, I think you might as well get it over with," said Celeste. "The more you try to avoid them, the more they'll be determined to hunt you down. Better they should talk to you here than come to our house."

"How would they find our house?"

"Callie, they're reporters. Eel found our house. Just go out there and answer their questions. You've already confessed. It's not like you have any beans to spill."

"I guess you're right." She sighed. "You know, if Haven were here, he'd march out there and lecture them until they ran for the hills. That's what I should do."

Celeste shrugged. "That's an idea. The best defense is a good offense."

"Is that how it goes? Or is it the other way? I can never remember."

"Doesn't matter. Just keep talking till they beg for mercy."

"Okay." Callie squared her shoulders and fluffed out her hair. "How do I look?"

"How do you want to look?"

"Scary."

"Hmm. Well. Honestly? Not even close. Try for something more in your range."

"Like what?"

Celeste studied her for a few seconds. "How about, 'radically deranged'?"

Callie frowned. She lifted her chin. "Come on. I want them to take me seriously."

Celeste shook her head slowly. "I don't think that's likely."

"Why not?"

"Look at you, you little freak. With that moon-maid hair and those starry eyes—you'd have better luck convincing them you're a total loon." She paused. "Maybe you should tell them you're the Goddess of Green Lake. They're gonna think you're nuts anyway."

"Thanks a lot. I don't want the story to be about me. I want them to write about Puki, about the whole otter situation." She thought for a minute. "How about if I call myself an otter liberator?"

"Sounds like a polka band."

"Puget Protector?"

"A condom."

Callie rolled her eyes. Celeste laughed.

"Don't worry about it, sweetie. It doesn't matter. Whatever you say they're going to misquote you and take things out of context."

"Well, that's comforting."

"Hey. You're the one who wanted to get on this merry-go-round. Don't blame me if you're dizzy."

"You're right. I'll just go out there and try to... sway them. With my powers. Of persuasion. How's that sound?"

"Very persuasive."

"Okay. Here I go."

As she stepped out into the sunlight, camera shutters and microphone switches clattered like mutant crickets before the door closed with a clunk and a tinkle of its bell.

After a half hour of talking to the reporters, Callie rode her bicycle home and collapsed on her bed. The nap she so desperately needed was less restful than she'd hoped, however, as a new crop of dreams opened in the theater of her subconscious—all thrillers. She kept starting awake feeling herself falling overboard far out at sea, or clutching at Eel as he fell out of a helicopter, or watching helplessly while Puki was devoured by an orca. She finally sat up, wiped the drool from her cheek, and checked the time. Almost five thirty. She went down to the kitchen to scrounge a dinner.

In the living room, Viola and Celeste were sitting on the couch watching a rerun of *That '70s Show*. Callie shuffled in and squeezed between them. After a minute she asked, "Can we watch the news?"

"You already missed it. We'll turn it back at six. You should check it out."

"Am I on it?"

"Oh boy. Are you ever," said Celeste.

"Is it bad?"

"It could be worse," said Viola.

"So it's not good."

"I didn't say that," said Celeste. "It's... entertaining."

Callie brought her knees up to her chest and frowned at the screen.

Viola looked over at her. "It's not that bad," she said. "They just kind of—"

"You look flakey," said Celeste.

"Flakey?"

"Flakey's not such a bad thing," Viola said. "You don't come across as evil."

Celeste nodded. "That's true. From a purely legal standpoint, you don't appear to be felon material."

"Just not completely..." Viola hesitated.

"Sane? Is that what you're saying? I look crazy?"

"Just wait. You can see for yourself. Besides, insanity's not a bad line of defense," said Celeste.

"I don't want to be committed."

"Don't panic. We could probably get custody," said Celeste.

"I don't know why I ever listen to you."

"Wait. Here it comes," said Viola, switching the channel.

The screen filled with footage of otters swimming, and a reporter's voice began, "These playful creatures once numbered in the thousands here in the Northwest, but ever since uncontrolled hunting wiped them out, the sight of sea otters has become increasingly rare in the region. Environmental activists have been working over the past two decades to reintroduce sea otters to Washington waters, and they've had some success. But not everyone agrees with their methods. Most recently, a pair of Seattle activists took matters into their own hands when they took a young sea otter from The Sounding's research program and released it into the wild."

Images of Eel being led off in handcuffs and Callie standing in front of the bakery flashed across the screen while the reporter briefly recounted the charges against them and the possible consequences. They only included one clip of Callie speaking, and taken out of context, the quote, "He was my baby and I had to set him free," sounded inane, even to her. When the focus shifted to an interview with a marine biologist who outlined the perils facing otters in the wild, Callie cringed. Before she had time to analyze her feelings, another voice filled the air.

"This deplorable incident should serve as a wake-up call to all those who truly care about the environment. This animal could have played an important part in the campaign to raise awareness about the environmental defense program. But now, thanks to the incompetence of a few people, we've lost another resource, lost time, lost funding, and in all likelihood the poor animal is already dead." Haven looked straight into the camera and continued, "As someone who has made it his life's work to protect the environment, I take this personally. These so-called activists have done more harm than good, and they deserve to be punished to the full extent of the law."

The reporter concluded the story with the date of the trial and a contact number for anyone with information about the missing otter.

Callie curled into a tight ball on the couch. Viola patted her on the back and said, "Hey. It doesn't matter what he says."

Callie picked idly at the chenille pillow next to her. After a moment she said, "What if he's right?"

"About what?"

"He could be dead already."

"Haven?"

Callie grimaced. "I know you're trying to make me feel better, but this isn't something you can fix. I don't know if we did the right thing. If Puki's dead... "

Celeste squeezed in beside her and wrapped her arm around Callie's slender shoulders. "Listen. You don't know. Puki could be miles away by now, drinking piña coladas in Santa Cruz."

Callie shook her head.

"Callie, this is only the start. Haven doesn't know any more than you do. He's just being Mr. Negative because that's what he does. It's his specialty. But you, you're something else, you understand? You are the shining, bright, sea girl—the otter liberator, remember? It's too soon to lose hope."

"She's right, you know," said Viola. "I mean, how many times have you gone out trying to find him?"

"Six times," Callie mumbled.

Viola nodded. "Okay. That's a start."

Callie sat quietly, unwilling to tell her sisters about the electricity she had felt in the water, when she had thought she had some kind of special ability to communicate with the otters. Now, with Haven's words ringing in her ears, she couldn't help wondering if she'd imagined the whole thing. Maybe she'd only been lucky before when she found the otters.

She closed her eyes and tried to remember the sensation she had felt so keenly in the boat, the sense of being connected to the otters, feeling their joy, their curiosity, their energy. She couldn't have imagined that, could she?

She sat up straighter. "You're right. There's a lot of water to explore still. And I don't have time to waste."

She got up and headed for the door.

"You're going now?" asked Viola. "It's almost dinner time."

"It'll be light for another three hours. I'll eat when I get back."

"What about practice?"

Callie stopped with her hand on the door knob. "Damn."

Celeste said, "Listen Callie, you can go out first thing tomorrow. We'll give you the week off. You can go out every day until you find him, okay? But the concert's important too. I mean... if you get fined a hundred thousand dollars..."

Callie frowned. "Guess we better hope the record goes platinum."

"That would help. Are we making a record?"

"No, but we should."

"I agree. So you need to come to practice."

"Okay, okay. I'm coming."

~ ~ ~

Blood in the water, blood in the vein
I am the sea's daughter, I live in the rain.
And now that I'm dying, what have you gained
With your mercury runoff and cruising disdain?
You slaughter my children, ignoring their pain.
Who gave you the ocean? What gives you the right
To murder its creatures, to profit from blight?
Will you find other worlds to ravage and raid
After the ruinous mess that you've made?
As if pumping sewage miles from the shore
Will stop it from killing the ocean's great store.
Close your eyes at your peril.
In time you must see.
It's killing you. It's killing me.
Blood in the water, blood in the vein
I am the sea's daughter, I live in the rain.

"Well, if that one doesn't fill the dance floor, I don't know what will," said Celeste.

"Yeah, it's a real toe-tapper," said Squid, grinning.

"You think it's too heavy?" Callie asked. "I mean, I know it's kind of lame but—"

"It's not lame. It's a protest song. People aren't supposed to dance to it." Eel nodded encouragingly at Callie. "Besides, anybody else here writin' any new songs?"

"We've got a couple more. They're not exactly protest songs," said Viola.

"That's okay. We need a lot of songs. Let's hear 'em," said Eel.

"Okay. Here's one we wrote especially for Callie," said Celeste, with a wink at Eel.

"Uh, oh," Callie muttered.

"It's called "Whatever Floats Your Boat.""

"I like it already," said Squid.

Viola sat beside him at the keyboard and said, "It goes like this."

Celeste sat next to her, and, after a few bouncing bars of syncopation, they began to sing in harmony.

Myrna was a girl with the sea in her eyes.
She fell for a sailor, to no one's surprise.
His muscles were brawny, his language was rough,
When he wrapped his arms around her,
She couldn't get enough.
But the sailor went to sea, as sailors always do
And Myrna had to wonder, if he would be true
Or would he find another, on some distant shore
Who would give him what he wanted,
And he always wanted more.
The months went by, he never called, he never sent a letter.
But Myrna read between the lines.
She knew she could do better.
She went down to the harbor, with her eyes open wide
Seeking a pirate to give her a ride.
Well it didn't take long to find a tattooed charmer

With a ring in his ear, a real disarmer.
He had a parrot, a monkey, a three-masted schooner.
When Myrna came aboard,
She wished she'd found him sooner.
They set off on the seas, higher than most,
And Myrna soon forgot her sailor in the arms of her host.
Whatever floats your boat, whatever fills your sail
Whatever rocks your world, whatever comes in the mail
Keep your head above water, and do like an otter:
Ride the waves with your baby in your arms.

"Woooh, wooh!" Duggan laughed. "That's great!"

"And it's danceable," said Eel.

Celeste looked at Callie. "What do you think?"

Callie grinned. "Are you kidding? It's the best ever! We should record that and sell it at the concert."

"Can we get it ready in time? We've only got a week," asked Viola, looking at Squid.

"No problem. I know some guys, who know some guys," he said.

For the rest of the practice, they focused on learning the song, and Callie's protest song, and another one of Eel's.

When practice wound up around midnight, Eel held Callie with a look, and she stayed behind after the others left. She told him of her plan to go out looking for Puki, and Eel insisted on going with her, even though she tried to put him off with her vague theory of sea magic.

"I think maybe I have to be alone for it to work," she said.

"I don't believe that, Callie. We found the otters together. They came when I was with you, remember? I'm not sayin' you don't have the goddess mojo. Because," he pulled her closer and dropped his chin to look steadily in her eyes, "I know you do. But I can help. You have to let me."

Heat rose in Callie's body, and she leaned into his arms. "Okay," she murmured. "We'll search the high seas together."

"Or, we could search the seas high together. If you like," he said.

She snorted softly and pulled away. "I'm paranoid enough already, thanks."

"What are you afraid of?"

She looked into his eyes, and stumbled slightly as a swirling sensation of dizziness nearly overcame her. He was standing right there in front of her, but she suddenly felt that inside himself he was far, far away.

CHAPTER EIGHTEEN

Callie and Eel spent the next three days sailing and searching until the sun dropped low in the sky. The first two nights the band rehearsed the new songs until they could play them blindfolded. The next night they went into the recording studio, and Squid assured them the CDs would be ready to sell at the concert Saturday night.

Singing with her sisters while Eel played behind her, Callie had moments of euphoria, but as soon as the music stopped, anxiety and guilt crashed into her consciousness again. She hid it as well as she could.

Only Eel noticed the shadow that lingered around Callie like a micro-climate of gloom. When the others had left after the recording session, Eel sat down beside her and waited.

"I have to go out alone," she said.

She didn't look at him, but started talking fast about the dream she had the night before. "It's not the first time I've dreamed about my mother. But it's been happening more often now. And the dreams are getting more real."

"They're still just dreams."

"Maybe." She bit her lip. "Last night she told me I have to go into the water to find Puki. She said I have to fulfill my destiny."

Eel shook his head. "Well, you know that's crazy, right? You can't breathe underwater. It's just a dream."

When she didn't answer, Eel shifted, trying to get her to look at him. "Listen Callie, you've got to have a little faith. We'll find him."

"What makes you so sure? Do you know what the odds are that he's been eaten or maimed? I was crazy to put him back out there."

"No you weren't. It was the right thing. Even your grandpa said so, didn't he?"

Callie frowned at the floor.

"Didn't he?" Eel persisted.

"I guess so."

"Maybe you should go talk to him again. Seems like he's not crazy at least."

Callie sighed. "Unlike me?"

Eel smiled gently. "There's good crazy and bad crazy."

She looked into his eyes. "And I'm...?"

"All good."

"I'm not all good," she whispered.

"And thank God for that," he said, leaning to kiss her.

For the next few days, the planet seemed to turn faster. Callie couldn't persuade Eel to let her go out alone on the Sound. Yet, something changed between them during the long hours in the boat. At first Callie didn't notice, but late in the afternoon on Friday she looked away from the water and watched Eel sitting quietly in the stern, staring out at the glittering sea. They hadn't spoken in what seemed like hours. As if he felt her eyes upon him, Eel looked at her, and the quiet confirmation in his gaze—like a steady flame—caught in her soul.

By the time they came in and tied up the boat she had made up her mind. The concert was the next day. The trial would begin on Monday. There was no more time for drifting.

She didn't say anything to him. There was no more time for arguing.

When they got to the community hall in Phinney Ridge people were lined up outside, waiting to get in. Callie pushed her way through to the door. The place was packed—standing room only. A blue spotlight trained on a mirror ball suspended overhead cast swirling splashes of color across the faces in the crowd. Callie had a moment of dizziness before Eel clasped her hand and charted a course to the stage.

Callie and her sisters opened the show. Clad in their shimmering gowns, they delivered a set of close harmonies and syncopated siren songs. The audience applauded wildly after every number. Between songs Callie spoke of the problems facing otters and the need for more environmental activism.

When Eel's unknown band took over, the audience listened to the first couple of songs with an air of suspended judgment until Squid kicked off a pulsing sea chantey. By the time Eel, Bob and Duggan joined in, layering the melody with counterpoint and harmony, a solid core of appreciative fans were wedged shoulder to shoulder at the front of the stage.

At the intermission, Eel announced that the combined band had just recorded its first CD of original material and no one would be allowed to leave without buying one. With that, the lights went down, the sisters stepped up, and the band opened the final set with "Blood in the Water." The crowd roared for more. They played Eel's song, "Cloud City Reel," and everyone gyrated as much as possible, considering they were packed in like crayons in a box. When Callie announced the last song, shouts of dismay rose from the dance floor. But as the band launched into "Whatever Floats Your Boat," the rocking mood lifted the crowd to new heights. They demanded an immediate encore, which the band provided, finishing with one of the Droplettes' sultry love songs. Sales of the new CD were brisk.

After the place had cleared out, Eel asked Tommy how much money they'd made.

"I won't know until we've had a chance to really do the numbers, but, offhand, I'd say we cleared maybe four thousand, including the CD sales. Not bad for a night's work," he said.

Eel nodded. "'S not enough. But's better than nothing."

"Hey. We'll sell more CDs too, don't forget," said Celeste. "We did great."

Eel gave Callie a ride back to her house. He was disappointed that she didn't want to stay with him. She told him she had to work early at the bakery, and she was completely exhausted from the week of searching and rehearsing.

"I'm glad tonight went well," she said, holding his hand. "But I really need a night in my own bed. Alone."

Eel rubbed his sunburned neck and stifled the desire that flared anew each time he looked at her, heard her voice, smelled her skin. "Okay," he said. "Call me when you wake up?"

She nodded, wondering if a nod counted as a lie.

The following morning, she slipped the tie line off and sat down at the tiller. The small outboard puttered as she eased the boat out of the marina. Rugby stood with his paws on the foredeck, sniffing the air, his tail wagging.

She hadn't planned to take him along, but when she was making her quiet pre-dawn getaway, Rugby had bounded after her, yapping with excitement. She was afraid he'd wake Celeste, so she hurriedly clipped his leash to his collar and jogged to the end of the block before she slowed down to walk the rest of the way.

There were other boaters out early on this Sunday morning. Few took notice of the girl and her dog. Once she cleared the crowded harbor, she cut the engine and raised the sail, heading north.

In the last two weeks, they had searched in vain all over the northernmost reaches of Puget Sound. This trip she aimed to search farther out in the Strait of Juan De Fuca.

A low cloud bank stretched across the distant horizon. The boat quickened in the strong breeze. She lost track of time as she sailed up the Sound; the scent of the sea lulled her anxiety. When the shoreline near Port Townsend came in view, she felt drawn to the vast waters beyond the strait, where the sea opened up. Rugby remained alert, looking out from the bow of the boat, his ears flapping in the wind. Occasionally he would glance back at her and give a happy bark. Callie was glad now she'd brought him along. Maybe he would sense something she couldn't.

She ate the sandwich she'd packed for the trip. The wind had picked up, and the wall of low clouds was rolling in from the west. Callie eyed them dubiously. Normally it didn't rain much in June. But this was a La Niña year, and normality is never all it's cracked up to be. As she headed in a westerly direction, the clouds thickened and the warmth in the air vanished. She was beginning to wonder if she should turn back, when a drop of rain hit her cheek. Rugby began to howl.

She frowned at him. "Hey, what's the matter with you? We love the rain, remember?"

Then she saw that Rugby was focused on something out in the water, and her heart skipped. She grabbed the binoculars, stood up, and trained them on the horizon. The water was getting choppier by the minute. At first she couldn't make out anything. But there was a darker speck. Too small to be a boat. Too far out to be a person.

She grabbed the tiller, shifted the sail, and tacked due west, right into the coming squall. The rain picked up, splattering steadily on her face and shirt. Callie grinned and muttered, "Wouldn't have it any other way."

An electric thrill coursed through her veins, as if she were picking up a signal from the very air. It had to be him. He was out there. She was sure of it.

The wind was gusting now. The sail rattled and snapped. She had to hold tight to the tiller to keep it from slipping out of her hands.

Rugby skittered on the wet deck. Callie hoped he wouldn't do anything stupid when they got to the otters. She had to get close enough to get a picture.

A crack of thunder split the clouds, and rain fell like a cold, dark wall, the sound drowning out everything else. Callie strained to keep the otters in sight. They were close enough now that there was no doubt. It was the raft. She tried to see if Puki was with them, but she couldn't catch up to them. She couldn't tell if they were moving away because of the storm or if the boat was being pushed back by the wind. They were getting farther away with every second. She stood up and shouted, "Puki! Puki!"

Her voice was lost in the swirling wind. She raised one hand and waved it frantically. A big wave slapped over the edge of the boat and knocked her to one side. While she struggled to regain her balance, another wave crashed over the boat and she lost her footing completely. Her head slammed against the edge of the hull, and she was swept over the side into the water.

Late afternoon sunlight glistened on the puddles when Eel parked his car in front of the house in Ballard. Impatient after waiting all day for her call, Eel had decided to surprise Callie by coming over instead.

He knocked on the screen door and heard footsteps approaching. Through the screen he saw a blonde figure, but this was not the blonde he was looking for.

"Hey. What brings you here?" asked Celeste, opening the door.

He stepped in. "Is Callie here?"

"I thought she was with you."

Eel frowned. "Did she say where she was going?"

"I haven't seen her all day. She was gone when I got up."

Eel stood still.

"Are you worried about her?" asked Celeste. "Don't be. She can take care of herself. She probably just went out in the boat.

Sometimes she needs to get away by herself on the water. It's a Callie thing."

"I know. 'S how she met me."

Celeste grinned. "That's right."

He looked back toward the door.

Celeste said, "Have you had dinner? You should stay. I'm sure she'll be here soon."

"I'm not hungry. Seems like she should be here. Trial starts tomorrow. She said she'd call me."

"Maybe she forgot. I know she's really worried about the trial. Maybe she went to see..." Celeste looked quickly at Eel's face and hesitated.

"That guy? Dudley DoRight?"

"Maybe."

Eel kept his mouth shut.

Celeste studied him. "She really cares about you, you know?"

"She cares about a lot of things."

"She cares about you. A lot."

"Not enough to tell me where she was going. I would have gone with her."

"Maybe she needed to be alone."

Eel looked past her into the room where light streaming through windows at the back of the house turned dust particles to gold shimmering in the still air.

A knock sounded at the door, abrupt as a gunshot. Celeste was first to reach the pair of policemen standing on the porch.

"Hello," one of the men said. "Is this your dog? We got this address from his tag."

The sight of Rugby, straining at the leash, hit Eel like a fist to his throat.

"That's my sister's dog," said Celeste, opening the door and taking the leash. Rugby jumped up and put his front paws on her shirt.

"Is your sister home?"

"No, she's been gone all day."

The other officer said, "We don't want to alarm you, Miss, but the dog was picked up along the north shore of Whidbey Island. The person who brought him in said he drifted in on a sailboat. Alone."

Celeste clutched Eel's arm.

"The boat was half full of water when it came in. There was a bad squall. The Coast Guard is searching the area now. If your sister got washed overboard, they may find her. If she was wearing a lifejacket."

Celeste gripped Eel's arm tighter.

"Is there anything we can do?" asked Eel.

"No. If your sister is... if she's drifting somewhere the Coast Guard will find her."

"Could she have washed up somewhere else?" asked Celeste.

"Anything's possible. She could have been picked up by someone else in another boat. Between Whidbey and the San Juans there are rocky shoals. She could have been carried some distance by the currents. If you hear from her, let us know," said the officer, handing Celeste a card.

The officers left. Celeste looked at Eel. His hand was on the doorknob.

"I can't just wait here," he said.

"You can't go now. It would be dark by the time you got up there. The Coast Guard knows the area. They'll find her. You have to be in court in the morning."

"So does she."

"Listen, I know you want to rush out there and rescue her. But you have to trust the Coast Guard to do its job. I'm sure Callie's fine. She'll probably show up here in an hour, wet and cranky and worried about Rugby."

"What if she doesn't?"

Celeste hugged him. "We'll get her back," she murmured.

"They'll find her," Viola assured him later, when she got home.

"She's an amazing swimmer," both the sisters told him.

They didn't tell him this had never happened before. Callie had never disappeared before. But their mother had. Though neither sister said it aloud, that fact hung in the air like a cold, choking gas.

CHAPTER NINETEEN

Callie gasped and coughed up saltwater as she clung to the slippery rock. The rain was still lashing the sea on all sides. Soaked through and cold to the bone, she knew she had to do something to warm herself up. The water temperature in the Sound, even in midsummer, seldom rose above fifty. After her short frantic swim to the relative safety of a small, rocky outcrop, her teeth were chattering uncontrollably. She had hoped to curl up next to some of the seals she had often seen basking on the rocks north of Whidbey, but none were around. She didn't dare jump up and down to keep warm; it was too slippery. She knelt at the edge of the slimy rocks and tore some strands of kelp loose and wrapped them around her body for insulation.

She couldn't see through the blinding curtain of rain. She had no sense of direction. Rugby was adrift who knows where. Her throat tightened at the thought of him barking helplessly as the boat was carried away. She hoped he would have the sense to stay in the boat until it reached shore. She prayed that it would reach shore. She pulled her knees in close to her body and huddled in the noisy, wet gloom, trying not to cry. She was wet enough already, she thought to herself with a grim little laugh.

For what felt like hours, she sat in the cold, slapping her hands against her body and listening to the storm slashing rain into the sea. Someone would come looking for her. Eventually. Once they figured out that she was gone. Her sisters would be angry. They wouldn't worry. But Eel—Callie felt strangled by regret as she considered what he would think when he learned she had gone without him, without telling him.

And as time passed, she couldn't avoid another stark realization. Alone and drenched in the stormy Sound, she felt no special connection to the sea. She was just cold and wet, like any ordinary human. She shivered and wiggled on the rock, trying to generate some heat. Glaring at the rain, which appeared to be letting up at last, she reached her hand out experimentally and patted the water at the edge of the rock. Nothing but wet.

Maybe my magic doesn't work during storms, she thought. *Or maybe it only works when Puki's around. Or...* she stared at the water, her shoulders drooping even as the clouds lifted. The air was growing lighter. But once it occurred to her, the thought wouldn't go away. What if the magic she had felt came from Puki? If it was magic. If she hadn't imagined the whole thing.

"Oh Callie, you're such an idiot," she muttered. "Did you honestly believe your mother? She was nuts. She only picked you to tell that story to because you were such a little sap. She knew you were the only one stupid enough to believe her."

A moment later, a bright ray of sunlight broke through the clouds and lit the rock behind her. Callie scowled at the sky and said, "Oh, come on. How gullible do you think I am?"

The wind had vanished by the time the Coast Guard patrol boat arrived, and the sun was slipping closer to the horizon. A seaman in a small inflatable raft helped Callie clamber on board and ferried her to the boat, where she was wrapped in a blanket and given a cup of hot cocoa. She stammered her thanks and apologized for being so foolish, but the crew didn't pay her much attention once they got her safely stowed. They seemed more intent on getting back to shore before nightfall. "You got a lot of people worried about you," one of the seamen said.

She wanted to ask who but felt that she'd caused enough trouble, so she bit her tongue and sat back, watching the lights on the shoreline. She wondered if Eel would be at the station waiting for her. More likely her sisters would be there. She contemplated the lecture she would have to endure. The lecture she deserved. She sighed softly and pulled the blanket closer around her body.

"Hey, cheer up. Not everyone gets rescued."

She looked up into the warm blue eyes of a young seaman.

"Yeah. I know. I just feel so stupid."

The young man shrugged. "Happens to everybody sooner or later. Don't worry about it." He looked at the rapidly approaching dock, then back at her, and asked casually, "What were you doing out there, anyway?"

"I was looking for something."

"Did you find it?"

"No. But I... I think I learned something."

The seaman nodded. "Well good. Don't forget it." He smiled and went to attend to the landing.

Callie looked past him. In the dim twilight, she saw someone standing on the dock. Her heart raced until she recognized who it was.

As the crew tied up the boat, she stepped onto the dock. Haven clasped her in his arms without a word. She was too tired to struggle, and for a moment just let herself sink into the security of his embrace, until he loosened his arms and looked down at her.

"I was afraid we'd lost you," he said.

She saw the tenderness in his eyes, and a spasm of resistance rose from her gut. She didn't want this.

Haven released his hold quickly, as if he'd read her thoughts.

"How did you—" she began.

"It was just a coincidence. I was down at the Coast Guard station this afternoon, monitoring the wildlife reports, and I heard them talking about a boat that washed ashore with a dog in it. I had this feeling, and then, when they brought Rugby in, I knew it was you. I wanted to go with them in the patrol boat, but they said I had to wait here." He looked at her carefully, reading her face until she turned away and looked at the floor.

After a slight pause, he said, "Callie, I know things have changed between us. I know you've found someone else. But even if you don't want... what I hoped we... what I'm trying to say is, I hope you'll let me be your friend. I hope you'll continue your work. That's what matters, you know."

Callie turned toward the Sound, where shore lights cast glittering reflections in the gathering darkness. "Yeah. I know," she said.

When Haven offered her a ride home, Callie felt it would be churlish to refuse. She made a quick call to let her sisters know she was on her way, and got in Haven's car.

They didn't talk much on the short ride. She was grateful that he seemed to understand that she was exhausted. When they reached the house, he said, "Are you okay?"

She gave him a little smile and said, "Yeah. I'll be all right. Thanks for..." She faltered, then leaned across the seat and gave him a quick hug and a kiss on the cheek before she got out of the car. As she walked up to the porch, she saw Eel standing in the shadows, watching her.

Callie slowed as she got close enough to see his face. She suddenly felt more afraid than she had when she was clinging to the cold, wet rock in the stormy sea.

"You told him, but you didn't tell me?" He spoke so softly she couldn't tell if he was hurt or angry.

"I didn't tell him."

"But you called him when you got back."

"I didn't! He just showed up at the dock. I went alone because I needed to go alone. I told you. And I didn't tell Haven anything."

He looked at her for half a minute. "You told me you had to work this morning. I guess that was a lie too."

She gaped at him, feeling not just his anger, but her own.

"Get over it," she snapped. "I nearly died out there. No lie. I'm sorry if I didn't take you along so you could have risked your neck too. We could have drowned together. Wouldn't that be romantic?" She stormed past him. He reached for her, but she jabbed him with her elbow. "Leave me alone. If you don't trust me..."

"Callie!" Celeste opened the door and pulled her inside where she was enveloped by a group sister hug.

"Don't ever do that again!" Viola said. "We were so worried."

"We were all worried," Celeste added, looking back toward the empty porch. She frowned at Callie. "He's been here for hours. Where did he go?"

"How would I know?" Callie mumbled. "I'm sorry for the trouble I caused."

Celeste eyed her tenderly. "You look like a drowned rat. But at least you're all right."

"You must be hungry," Viola said. "Come on, you should eat."

"I don't feel like eating," Callie said. Her gut was still churning from the sting of Eel's accusation. She turned back to the porch and looked outside. There was no sign of him.

Celeste came up beside her. "Don't pay too much attention to what he said. He's been worried sick. He's probably sorry already. You guys are both so stressed out. And tomorrow..."

Callie hung her head. "Yeah. Tomorrow."

"Have you thought about what you're gonna wear?"

Callie snorted softly. "I can honestly say that's one thing I haven't thought about at all."

"Well, don't worry. We'll fix you up. Make you look like a respectable citizen."

They sat in the kitchen. Callie ate leftover salmon while her sisters discussed courtroom fashion and etiquette. As soon as the food hit her stomach she was so tired she could hardly sit up.

"Uh, oh, looks like the Little Mermaid is losing her legs," Viola said.

"Come on sweetie, let's get you to bed," Celeste said.

Callie passed out as soon as her head hit the pillow. And for once, she was too tired to dream.

Across town, Eel couldn't face going up to the apartment. He didn't want to talk to anyone, or listen to anyone. He tried not to think about the sight of Callie hugging her old boyfriend. He tried not to think about how swiftly the happiness he'd felt on seeing her return had been shattered by a few harsh words.

He tried not to think at all.

The next morning a small crowd gathered in front of the courthouse. Eel, wearing a relatively clean, long-sleeved dress shirt and black jeans, stood with Tommy and Abby, Squid, Fergus, and Alice, who held the wide-eyed baby. When Callie approached, flanked by her sisters, she stared at the group. For an instant she wondered if the couple with the small child were Eel's relatives. The older olive-skinned man bore a strange resemblance to Eel.

As she came closer, she thought she detected a new shadow in Eel's usually impassive expression. She quickened her pace. She gave him a quick hug and whispered, "You look nice."

He shrugged, and she felt the tension in his body. She cast a questioning look at the couple standing with Tommy and Abbie. Eel introduced them briefly as old friends.

"We came to support Eel," Alice said.

"And you too, of course," added Fergus. "Any friend of Eel's... " He shot a quick smile at Eel, who didn't respond.

The courthouse doors opened.

"Showtime," said Celeste.

The crowd bustled into the building, lined up for bag inspections, and went through the metal detectors. Soon they were seated in the courtroom, where conversations had to be conducted in whispers.

Eel and Callie sat next to their lawyer, who bent his head closer and told them he had a new plan for their defense. Before he had time to say more, the judge banged his gavel and the room fell silent.

The prosecution delivered a swift but thorough summation of the case and the charges against Eel and Callie. Since both the defendants had pled guilty, the case was clear, he claimed.

Dwight Chubb opened the defense, calling his first witness, Ms. Strathorn, The Sounding's top administrator. Chubb first asked her a series of routine questions about how she met the defendants. He then asked her to recall the events of the day when Callie brought Puki to The Sounding.

While Ms. Strathorn spoke, the lawyer nodded agreeably. But when she finished, he looked puzzled.

"Maybe I missed something in your story, Ms. Strathorn. By your account, the defendant found an orphaned wild animal, which she rescued from the wild because she thought it was too young to survive alone. Is that right?"

"That's what I said," said Ms. Strathorn.

"I see. And you, that is The Sounding, agreed to care for the animal?"

"Yes."

"And did you give Ms. Linden any money? In exchange for the animal?"

Ms. Strathorn frowned. "Of course not. She didn't sell it to us."

"So, you considered the animal a gift?"

Ms. Strathorn shifted in her chair. "No. The Sounding has always provided a safe environment for distressed or injured creatures. It's part of our mission, along with educating the public."

"I see. So this wild animal was in your care, but never legally belonged to you, or I should say, The Sounding. You were simply boarding it, as it were."

Ms. Strathorn's frown lines grew deeper. "Inasmuch as the animal was in our care, we considered it our responsibility. And we take our responsibilities very seriously. Our primary goal is to do what's best for the animals."

Chubb nodded. "Of course. But the animal in question, this young otter, had been removed from its natural habitat and placed in an artificial environment. Would you agree that accurately describes the situation?"

"What are you getting at?" asked Ms. Strathorn testily. "Puki was a well-adjusted resident of the facility until that man began playing music at him."

A murmur went through the courtroom.

Chubb raised his eyebrows.

"Ms. Strathorn, The Sounding charges admission, isn't that right?"

"Of course. It costs a lot to maintain the facility, and to provide the level of care that we do."

"And yet, if you had no animals, people wouldn't pay to go there."

Ms. Strathorn said, "What's your point?"

"The point is, Ms. Linden brought a valuable creature to The Sounding and left it in your care. She received no compensation for her efforts, even though The Sounding benefited from the creature's presence."

Ms. Strathorn bridled. "We certainly don't make money off the animals in our care. It costs a small fortune to provide for them. We have to charge admission to survive."

"I see. So that's why you couldn't afford to pay Ms. Linden for her otter."

"We don't pay for animals! And it wasn't her otter either!" Ms. Strathorn's voice rose.

"So you admit it wasn't yours?" Chubb's lips tightened in a slight smile as he turned to pull a folder of papers from the pile on the desk behind him.

"Your honor, I have here copies of Sounding records which clearly show that, as a matter of fact, The Sounding buys nearly all of the creatures in its exhibits with the exception of a few cases where injured or orphaned animals have been donated to the facility." He handed the file to the judge and then turned back to Ms. Strathorn, who was glaring at him stonily.

"In view of the fact that The Sounding never purchased the otter in question, and that the defendant never signed any formal documents transferring ownership of the creature to The Sounding, I put it to the court that in setting free this creature of the wild, no crime has been committed."

A fresh breeze of whispers kicked up in the courtroom. The judge banged his gavel. When order was restored, he asked both lawyers to approach the bench.

"Mr. Chubb, your clients have been charged with a class C felony. That's a serious charge. They have both already pled guilty to the charges against them. The purpose of this hearing is not to decide whether they have committed a crime, but how severely they will be punished. Do you understand that?"

"Yes, your honor. I do. And that's why I think it's important to recognize that, although my clients have been charged with releasing an animal, the prosecution cannot prove that the animal was the legal property of the facility, and thus my clients were acting within the law when they removed the animal and returned it to its original home."

"This is nonsense!" hissed the prosecuting attorney.

The judge grimaced and sighed heavily. "I don't suppose you two could work out an agreement that would shorten this process?"

"Your honor, my clients would be happy to let the whole matter drop. They are not crusading to free all zoo animals. They simply wanted to return this one young otter to its home."

"This is ridiculous!" the prosecuting attorney snapped. "These punks broke into a private educational facility and removed a valuable exhibit. It doesn't matter whether it was an otter or a moon rock. They broke the law and they deserve to be punished."

The judge turned to Chubb and said, "Counselor, I am going to allow you to continue, but I warn you, this isn't Boston Legal. I won't allow you to make a mockery of this court."

"I have no intention of doing so, your Honor. I'm just trying to keep innocent creatures from being locked up."

"I hope you're referring to your clients," said the judge.

"Them too," said Chubb.

As the tedious legal origami unfolded around her, Callie's thoughts turned again and again to the older couple who had come in support of Eel. Several times during the long morning Callie caught Eel exchanging a glance or a half-smile with one of his allies. The link between Eel and the older man mystified her. She sensed Eel's respect for Fergus, and something more than that.

When the court adjourned for lunch, the whole group—Eel and his supporters, Callie and her sisters, and Finn, Celeste's latest boyfriend–in–training, went to a restaurant on First Avenue. While they waited for their orders, Callie squeezed Eel's hand beneath the table and said, "Well, so far, so good, I guess."

He shrugged. Callie let go of his hand and stared at him. He looked back at her and said quietly, "Didn't see your boyfriend in the courtroom."

She pursed her lips. "Maybe he's out on the Sound with his reporter friend, trying to help us."

"Sure. Tryin' to help 'us'."

Callie murmured, "You should be thankful anyone wants to help us."

Eel looked across the table at Alice, who returned his gaze with a warmth that puzzled Callie .

Alice turned to Squid and said, "So, Squid, how do you like Seattle? Tommy tells me you came up from California too."

"'S kinda wet. Music scene's pretty good though. Not so many phonies as in LA." He paused, and looked at Eel. "We got a gig tonight. If Eel's not locked up."

"Speaking of locked up," said Tommy, "what happened to the publicity for your case? I haven't seen much in the papers."

Callie shook her head. "They wrote about it when it first happened, but since then, you know, reporters have short attention spans. If the story's not about something really gruesome, they lose interest. But we might be getting some publicity soon. A friend of mine is trying to get a reporter from the Times to do a story on the sea otters and the problems they face."

"I was thinking about the bigger picture," Tommy said. "You know, when we were fighting for my mom's garden in Virginia, nobody cared until Fergus got everyone's attention, and then the worldwide media got involved, and ultimately that's what saved the garden."

Callie looked at Eel. "You fought for a garden?"

"Was a really nice garden. Had turtles and everything," he said.

Callie turned an inquiring eye to Alice.

"I made a garden on an empty lot that wasn't mine," Alice explained. "When a developer bought the lot and was going to pave over the garden, Fergus came and helped me protect it." She smiled at Tommy and Eel. "Everyone helped."

Callie shook her head. "I don't understand. How did you get the media's attention?"

"Go ahead, Green Man. Tell her," Eel said, looking at Fergus.

The older man shrugged and said, "You might not believe it, but I was once a Green Man." He paused, as if waiting to see if Callie recognized the term, but before she could respond Celeste said, "Hey, Finn's a Green Man too!"

Fergus looked intently at the lean young man sitting close to Celeste and raised an eyebrow. "Is that right?" he asked.

Finn nodded. "Yeah. I'm a tree guy."

Fergus lowered his voice and said, "You're from The Realm?"

Finn frowned slightly. "The what?"

Fergus leaned back. "That's what I thought."

Celeste said, "Finn's a great tree man. I hired him to do some work on our chestnut and it looks better than ever."

"I'm glad to hear it." Fergus looked at Finn. "So you're in the business?"

Finn sat up straighter. "Yeah. I'm a professional. You too?"

"Not anymore. I'm just an ordinary landscaper now."

"There's nothing ordinary about you," said Alice, kissing him on the cheek.

Finn looked from Fergus to Eel and asked, "Are you two related?"

Eel ducked his head and eyed Fergus, who was clearly enjoying this turn in the conversation. They replied simultaneously.

"No," said Eel.

"Yes," said Fergus.

Callie stared from one to the other.

Fergus cleared his throat. "You could say we share the same family tree."

Eel smiled. "Yeah. That's it."

Tommy turned to Callie and said, "Haven't you ever heard of Green Men? They've been around for centuries. They work to protect everything in nature."

Abby added, "You see pictures of them at festivals and garden centers. There's sculptures of them all over the churches in Europe. The face in the leaves?"

Callie nodded uncertainly.

Viola said, "So, you're saying that Fergus is one of those kind of Green Men?"

Tommy and Abby and Eel all nodded.

"Wow," said Finn. "Pretty cool, dude."

Fergus lost his air of amusement and said in a more serious tone, "Green Men aren't charged with preventing all harm... only with protecting the magical trees which serve as portals between this world and the other. My tree was in Alice's garden."

"Was?" asked Callie.

"Alice's former husband destroyed it during the struggle. But Alice was able to restore the garden, thanks to the seed we had planted."

Alice smiled at the toddler in her lap.

"Oh," said Callie. "But—"

"Trees take time. I lost my immortality when my tree was destroyed. What magic I possessed is also gone."

"Oh I wouldn't say that," said Alice.

Fergus bowed his head in her direction. "I think what Tom is trying to say is that if you want to help the otters, you have to cast your net wider than just around Seattle, or even the West Coast. Allies can be found worldwide."

"He's right," said Celeste. "I know you said Grandpa discouraged you from trying to use a picture to sway public opinion. But Grandpa's out of touch. What you need is a kick-ass YouTube video."

"Right," said Tommy. "If we could get some footage of Puki— maybe use one of Eel's songs with it—that could get the kind of publicity that makes a difference."

"We've been trying to find him for weeks," Callie said. "But he seems to have disappeared."

No one said anything. Then they all started talking at once.

"You need a website for raising money—"

"Anything that makes people more aware—"

"Where can we find otters?"

"Maybe I should just go to Canada."

"Hey! You're not going anywhere," Callie's voice rose above the rest and heads turned their way in the restaurant.

Viola looked at her watch and said, "Yeah, about that? We should be getting back."

The second half of the court procedure went more quickly than the first. In spite of their lawyer's attempt to make the case that no crime had been committed, Callie and Eel saw nothing encouraging in the judge's increasingly impatient demeanor. When Chubb tried to call Fergus to the stand as a character witness for Eel, the judge cut him short, saying, "Counselor, we are not here to judge the defendants on their personal character. This is a case of *facta non verba*. There's no dispute about what actions your clients took. I suggest you have mercy on this courtroom and spare us the song and dance."

Following this remark, Chubb shook his head at Eel and Callie, and finished up with a brief, impassioned plea for lenience, given the youth and prior clean records of the defendants. When he finished, the judge said, "In view of the evidence before me, and in the interest of not wasting more time or taxpayer money, I'm prepared to deliver a sentence without further delay.

"While it appears that these defendants acted with good intentions, the court does not accept the defense's suggestion that no crime was committed. In the view of this court, an implicit transfer of ownership of the animal took place when Miss Linden left the creature at The Sounding. Coupled with the fact that the defendants illegally entered the facility after hours and removed the animal, this constitutes a clear case of an act against an animal facility. I find the defendants guilty on all charges and order them to pay the plaintiff all costs of this litigation, including attorney's fees and court costs, and in light of the gravity of this case and the danger of inspiring similar crimes, I am imposing a civil fine of twenty thousand dollars to be paid to the plaintiff, and I am sentencing each of you to two years' probation."

The judge looked directly at Callie and Eel. "Just to clarify, that's twenty thousand from each of you." He banged the gavel and dismissed them with a wave of his hand.

Callie stood, numb with shock, until Celeste grabbed her arm and said, "Come on, let's get out of here."

She looked around for Eel and felt a rush of panic when she didn't see him. She pushed to get through the crowd.

Outside the courthouse, the sisters paused with Callie between them. Viola said, "Do you want to go someplace with Eel and his friends?"

Callie caught sight of him then. He was walking down the steps toward her. Behind him, Tommy, Abby and Squid waited with Fergus and Alice.

"I need to talk to you," he said.

She stepped away from her sisters. Eel turned and walked a few steps farther, out of earshot of his friends or hers. Then he turned to face her.

"Well," she said, "That wasn't so good."

"Could have been worse," he replied.

"How? You mean jail with no option?"

"Listen, Callie, I been thinking about this a lot—"

"Me too."

"I know. But... now... " He paused, squinting at the sunlight in the clear blue sky. "I gotta get a job. Maybe two. Or three. I don't know how I can pay this off."

"They'll give us time. They can't expect us to pay it all at once."

"I don't know about that. But I do know we can't be... you need to be... and I've got to—"

"I know. But it's okay as long as we're together." She tried to meet his eyes, but he turned away, looking back at Fergus.

"I don't know," he said. "Maybe we were never meant to be together." He looked at her and turned away quickly, as if the sight hurt his eyes. "I'm sorry." And with that he turned and walked swiftly to his friends, who surrounded him as they went away.

Callie's heart stuttered as she watched him disappear. She felt a ringing pressure in her ears. Everything seemed far away, muffled by the roar of her emotions.

"What did he say? Are you all right?" Viola was at her side, wrapping an arm around her shoulders.

Callie heaved a choking sob. "I don't want to talk about it."

CHAPTER TWENTY

Callie crumpled another tissue and tossed it on the pile beside her bed. She shut her swollen, red eyes and fell back on her pillow.

"You know what I don't get? That whole thing that women are the romantic ones. That men are supposedly all tough and hard and couldn't care less about sappy stuff. That all they care about is sex and sports. What a crock! Men are marshmallows. All that tough talk and fighting and nastiness is just a huge smoke screen to cover the fact that they really really really want someone to love them, and they're so afraid of rejection that they'd rather die than admit it. Or go to jail. Or run away. I could scream."

She looked at Celeste, who was leaning against the door.

"I know I've got to get over this," Callie said. "It just pisses me off when I think how I was mean to Haven. Not that that's Eel's fault, but if he hadn't come along none of this would have happened. I never would have had the guts to steal Puki if he hadn't helped. And now they're both gone."

Celeste sat on the edge of the bed. "You know he's just upset. He really loves you. He'll probably call tomorrow and say he's sorry."

Callie sniffed. "I don't know. Maybe he's right. Maybe he's bad for me, and I'm bad for him. Look what a mess we made of things. Puki's out there somewhere, in more danger than he was before. The Sounding has lost a ton of money, and now we have to come up with thousands of dollars. And for what? What good was all of this?"

"Come on. You're just tired. It's been a rough couple of days. Things will look better in the morning."

"People always say that. But you know? It's not true. Things are going to look even worse tomorrow. He's not going to call. I know he's not. Even if he does love me, he thinks he's doing what's best for me. Aaaagh! Why do men always think they know what's best for me? Haven's just the same. Always telling me what to do, what to think. They can't tell me how I feel."

Celeste smiled. "That's right. They can't. But I can. And right now you're tired. So I'm going to turn out the light, and you're going to go to sleep, and when we get up tomorrow, we'll figure out how to raise the money, and then, after we've done that, you can decide how you feel on the subject of boyfriends."

"Bah. Boyfriends."

"Yeah, I know. Can't live with 'em, no fun without 'em."

As Celeste shifted to get up, Callie grabbed her wrist. "Thanks, Cele," she muttered. "I won't be such a whiney baby tomorrow. I promise."

"Good. Because I've about shot my wad of patient sisterhood. I need to get back to my natural state."

"The carefree bitch?"

Celeste stood up and smiled. "You know me well."

"I wonder if I could pull that off," Callie muttered.

Celeste paused at the door and looked back at her fondly. "I don't know, Cal. You have to be who you are."

"Huh. I'm not sure who that is anymore."

"Goodnight sweetie."

"I'm not sweet!"

Celeste laughed as she closed the door.

Eel didn't call in the morning. Or later that day. Or the next. Callie was hurting, but she set herself to recover her once-firm conviction of who she was and what her goals were. And in nurturing this personal rebuild, she found a steady ally in Haven.

At first, when he called and offered her a paying job, she declined, leery of emotional entanglement and lofty lectures. But Haven surprised her with his unwavering support. And he was tactful about the money. She understood that his eagerness to help her pay off the fine was his way of demonstrating faith in her. Still stinging from the pain of Eel's abrupt exit, she appreciated the feeling of being valued by someone she respected. Haven continued to fight the good fight, even though his own brief day in court hadn't brought about the results for which he'd hoped.

He urged Callie to give up her job at the bakery and devote every available hour to the cause. Callie's sisters agreed that it would be a constructive step for her. They could manage the bakery without her.

Eel got a job with a nursery/landscaping business in West Seattle. The early hours and long days took some getting used to, and the physical labor gave him calluses in new places, but he found the work surprisingly satisfying. Taking truckloads of plants and transforming sites into pleasing compositions of form, mass and light gave Eel a sense of accomplishment he hadn't felt before. It was nothing like playing music for a live audience, but on the other hand, the work didn't vanish into thin air as soon as he finished. The idea that gardens grow more beautiful with time was strangely soothing.

As he worked, he tried to focus on the leaves, willing himself to see inside the living things as Fergus had suggested. But he felt pressured to work quickly. The rest of the crew went about their tasks smoothly and steadily, with no hesitation, no contemplative pauses, and Eel had to keep up. By the end of each day, he was too physically spent to bother trying to read between the leaves.

Meanwhile, Squid was having success booking the new band. Often when Eel came home ready for a beer and some rest, he had to pick up his guitar and go out to play at some club. He didn't mind.

Better to be too busy than not busy enough. It kept him from dwelling on thoughts of Callie.

In early July, Squid and Duggan found a house for rent in Alki, and Eel gave up his apartment and moved across the city. The house was closer to his day job, and the band had gotten a steady gig at one of the bars on the beach strip. He was beginning to hear new songs in his head. Some, with titles like "Shipwrecked," "Shoal Man" and "Can't Fathom You," came directly out of his misery. Yet the combination of exhausting physical labor by day and musical collaboration by night fostered a renewal of hope. He wasn't ready to call Callie, but he began to imagine a time when he could.

One night in late July, when Squid and Duggan had gone out to pursue another gig, Eel stayed behind to work on song ideas. Alone in the sparsely-furnished living room, he stared out the bay window overlooking the Sound. Sunlight poured in, backlighting a row of small plants Eel had brought home from the nursery. After nearly a month of trying to get a response from anything green, he had pretty much written off the idea of his so-called magic. Maybe the Green Man had been mistaken. Maybe he'd imagined the music he heard in the forest.

He gazed at the setting sun while he played riffs on his guitar, and as the light in the room faded, he hit upon a melodic line that held his interest. He closed his eyes to concentrate, allowing his fingers to explore the mood of the song in his head. After a while, he stopped and opened his eyes in the dark room. He gaped at the plants on the windowsill. A strange, green glow shone from their leaves. They shimmered like living candles. Eel stared until his eyes watered. Gently, he plucked a string on the guitar. The light in the plants pulsed brighter. He strummed a chord. They pulsed brighter still. He shook his head and murmured, "Are you kidding me?"

The green radiance from the plants cast an otherworldly spell on the room, giving it the ambience of some fairytale forest den. Eel began to play a new song, watching the plants as he did. The lights grew brighter in time with the music, and when he stopped, the plants continued to glow. Eel looked at the clock. How long would this last? And what good was it? Would they still be glowing when Squid and Duggan returned? Were the leaves like batteries, absorbing musical energy? Questions and conjectures were burning in Eel's brain long after Squid and Duggan returned with news of a tentative gig on a party boat. The plants had stopped glowing by then, and the guys didn't seem quite as dazzled by Eel's discovery as they were by their own. Eel had to admit that the practical applications of glow-in-the-dark plants were limited. So he filed it away for later investigation and joined in the discussion of the potential for seasickness playing on a boat.

Callie was less successful in her not-thinking-about-Eel effort. Although the new job with Haven's Sound Sense organization demanded long hours and focused attention, she was unable to put Eel out of her thoughts. She missed the sound of his voice, the sight of his face, the ineffable sense of rightness that came over her whenever she was near him. She had trouble sleeping and took to helping out at the bakery in the predawn hours.

One rare, hot night in late July, as Callie lay on top her bed, trying not to sweat in the non-air-conditioned closeness of her upstairs room, Viola knocked gently on the door frame. "You okay?" she asked.

Callie sighed. "Yeah. Just melting."

"Want the fan?"

"Nah. Maybe I can sweat out some of the misery."

"You're still miserable?"

"Kind of."

"About?"

"Oh, you know. I got a list."

"What's number one?"

Callie sat up and wrapped her arms around her knees. "It's just... It's been four weeks. I thought he'd figure it out by now."

"That he can't live without you?"

"Right. Shouldn't he have?"

Viola came over and sat on the edge of the bed. "Maybe. Maybe he really believes he's not good enough for you."

"That's ridiculous."

Viola shook her head. "I don't know, Cal. He's only a guy."

"I'm only a girl."

"I thought you were a magic mermaid. That's a lot of pressure for the average guy to deal with."

"Eel's not average."

Viola nodded. "I know. Maybe you need to go see him and remind him."

"Do you think? I don't want to be pushy."

"If he's feeling insecure, he's not going to make the first move."

"You think I should?"

"I don't think it would hurt." Viola stood up and went to the door. She paused there and looked back at Callie.

"What?" Callie asked.

Viola shrugged. "I just wondered if that was all."

"What do you mean?"

Viola gazed at her steadily. "You know. Sometimes I think about how all of this started with you finding that otter, and... it just seems like things kind of got crazy. I guess I've been wondering if you ever had any second thoughts about... the whole thing. I mean, I never saw your otter. Was it worth all of this?"

Callie closed her eyes and grew very still.

Viola backpedaled. "I'm sorry, if that was out of line—"

"No." Callie shook her head rapidly. "No, it's not out of line. I've thought about it a thousand times. But I can't describe how I felt except to say... when I was with Puki... I felt like I was connected to Mom." She stared at Viola. "I know that sounds crazy... but... that's

184

what it was like for me. There was something so special about him. And it wasn't just me, either. It was Eel, too. Puki connected with Eel." Callie shook her head. "When I hear myself say that, it sounds crazy even to me. But... that's what it was. It was like, the whole time—when I was with Puki, when we were looking for him—I felt as if I was feeling something that Mom would have understood. Not love, exactly. It was like this... joy. Just being glad to be alive, to be connected with something bigger than yourself. And at the same time feeling helpless because you know you can't protect anyone or anything from danger. Not forever anyway." She sighed. "I tried."

Viola stared at her. "Mom would have been proud of you."

"Maybe she is."

Viola smiled. "Yeah. Maybe."

Two days later, Callie rode the bus over to the U District and got out in front of Eel's building. She felt clammy with sweat, and uncertain about what she was going to say. She hurried up the walk and into the building. After climbing the three flights of stairs, she was even sweatier, and starting to have doubts, but she'd come this far and wasn't about to back down. She knocked on the door and held her breath.

There was music coming from inside the apartment. It didn't sound like anything Eel would play. The door was opened by a gum-chewing, barefoot, halter-top-wearing brunette, who gave Callie a blank look. "Yeah?" she said.

Callie blinked. "I'm looking for Eel MacGregor?"

"Who?"

Callie felt as if the floor had dropped out from under her. "Do you live here?" she asked.

"Yeah," the girl said.

"Did you just move in?"

"Two weeks ago."

"Do you know what happened to the guys who were here before you?"

"Not a clue." The girl leaned against the doorway, chewing her gum.

"Okay. Thanks. Sorry to bother you."

The girl shut the door without another word. Callie went down the stairs slowly. She didn't know whether she was more sad or angry. By the time she got home anger had won out.

She stomped through the living room. Viola asked, "How'd it go?"

"I'm over it," Callie said. She strode to the back of the house and grabbed Rugby's leash. "I'm going for a walk."

"Did you have a fight?"

Callie paused on the doorstep. "No. You can't fight with someone who's disappeared. But trust me, if he shows up again, he'd better be ready." She went out and slammed the door. A moment later she cracked it open and said, "Sorry about that. It just felt like the right thing to do. I didn't mean it to you."

"I know, sweetie. Have a good walk."

As she marched down the sidewalk toward the Sound, Callie's anger fizzled. She couldn't really blame Eel for moving on. She just wished he'd told her where he was going. At the end of the street, where the Sound opened wide and bright, like a gateway filled with promise, she stared at the water and confronted what was really bothering her.

Ever since the storm and those cold, miserable hours she'd spent huddled on the kelp-covered rock, Callie had avoided dealing with her sense of failure, hoping it would subside with the passage of time. But the notion that she was nothing more than a deluded girl who had made a bad decision dug into her, like a thorn in her skin. There was no way to undo what she'd done. Puki was at the mercy of the sea now.

She sat on a bench and watched Rugby sniffing around the rocks, reading them the way her grandfather read the waves.

That thought launched ripples of regret. She hadn't gone to see him since the trial. She knew he'd forgive her for being stupid, but she couldn't bear to see disappointment in his eyes.

She called Rugby. The little dog bounded to her, his ears flapping like pennants. "Okay, pal," she said. "Let's go see Grandpa."

She found him, smoking his pipe on the back porch.

He eyed her carefully before he spoke. "You must have quite a speech for me."

Callie faltered. "What?"

"I figured the reason you've been staying away was you were working on your speech. The one about how hard you tried and how sorry you are and so on."

Callie bit her lip. "I don't have a speech."

"Going to be a quiet visit then."

"What do you mean?"

"I don't have a speech either."

Callie almost smiled. "I don't know what to say, Grandpa. I thought... I thought I knew... I..." She paused and frowned. Then she stared into his eyes. "Am I really like my mother?"

He studied her face. "In what way?"

"She told me she was a mermaid. That that's why she had to leave us." Callie kept her eyes on the old man. "You knew, didn't you?"

He shrugged. "I knew your mother had fanciful ideas. I don't know if they were more than that. Or if she told herself those things to make it all right to do what she wanted. No matter the cost."

"Am I like her?"

"In some ways."

Callie frowned and leaned closer, lowering her voice. "I think I always wanted to believe Mama was special, and that, because of that, I was special too. But when I was out there, alone, in the storm, I tried to reach out to the sea." She shook her head. "I know that sounds stupid, but I had these feelings before... when I was alone on the water."

"What kind of feelings?"

"When I touched the water. I thought it was responding to me. Like an electric pulse or something. Does that sound insane?"

Grandpa Linden tapped his pipe out. "Callie, I'm an old man, and I've seen a lot of things on the water, and felt a lot of things too. I've never felt anything like you describe, but I'm not such a fool that I'd say it couldn't happen. There's a world of mysteries in the sea. Could be it's for you to discover them."

Callie started to fidget. There was only one question she really wanted answered. "Is it possible that I'm some kind of mermaid?"

He smiled and leaned back in his chair. "Did she tell you that?"

She nodded. "She said I couldn't tell anyone else."

He shook his head. "Your mother was a great beauty. But you're more than that. You're smarter than she was. Smart enough to survive in a stormy sea."

Callie hung her head. "I was afraid."

"Proves you're not a fool."

"But ...?"

"Callie, I don't know anything about mermaids, but your mother was born with two legs like the rest of us." He paused and looked at her steadily. "I'm sorry she ran away. But you, now, you're a natural born sireen, strong and true. You do good work in this world. I'm proud of you, just the way you are."

"But we've lost Puki, and I don't know if we'll ever know what happened to him."

"Well. Not all mysteries are meant to be solved. It doesn't matter whether you ever find him. What matters is that you keep your eyes open. Who knows what you might find?"

A week later, Callie was drinking a cup of coffee and reading the newspaper, fighting a growing sense of outrage over a story about a cruise ship that had recently arrived in Vancouver with a dead seventy-foot whale impaled on its hull. The captain and crew claimed they had no idea when they'd struck the whale and tried to suggest that it had been dead when they hit it, as if to absolve themselves of blame. Callie was sputtering with fury as she turned the page, but she nearly gagged on her doughnut when a different article caught her eye. The headline read: "Scuba Divers Discover Giant Kelp Forest Near Port Townsend."

She scanned the article quickly, then read it again slowly. It said that a pair of amateur scuba divers had stumbled onto an unexpected and unprecedented forest of giant kelp in one of the deep channels east of Port Townsend. The significance of the find could not be overstated, since giant kelp was normally found only in the waters off California. Unlike the common, shorter, bull kelp, which dies back each winter, giant kelp is a perennial that can live up to seven years and grow to a length of one hundred feet, forming huge, underwater forests, which nurture whole ecosystems of marine life. And sea otters are the keystone species in the kelp forest system. The otters' natural diet of sea urchins is vital in preserving the balance, since sea urchins devour kelp.

Callie's pulse quickened as she thought of what this could mean in the fight to protect the Sound's marine life. She wondered if somehow Puki was connected to the sudden appearance of giant kelp where none had ever been seen before. If giant kelp could get established in the Sound, maybe sea otters could regain their place in the Sound too.

According to the map in the article, the giant kelp forest was located perilously close to one of the channels used by some of the Seattle-based cruise ships.

Callie jumped to her feet, tore off her apron, said a quick goodbye to her sisters, and hurried to the office. When she got there, Haven and the rest of the staff were already debating how to use the discovery to launch a new campaign.

"We'll need to have it verified by the scientific community before we can try to get new legal protections in place," said Haven.

"We can't wait," said Callie. "That could take months. All it takes is for one cruise ship to plow through there and the kelp will be gone. And so will the otters."

"I know, Callie. But we don't have the resources to stop the cruise ships. The Clean Cruise Ship Act, even if it passes someday, won't stop them. If it were only a handful of ships, we might be able to put up some kind of blockade, the way Greenpeace shields the whales. But this isn't 1999. More than two hundred cruise ships are scheduled to come through our waters this season."

Callie's eyes blazed. "So, what? Are we just giving up? We've got to take a stand, now! This is our chance."

"I agree. But, realistically Callie, how do you propose we do that? I'll try anything."

The staff began talking about the high cost of television spots, the value of bus posters, internet buzz.

"Too bad we can't get a video of the forest and put it on YouTube," said Ryan, one of the interns.

Callie rolled her eyes. "Why is it every time there's a problem people think the answer is on the internet? YouTube is for dancing cats and stupid politicians. This isn't entertainment. This is life and death. We have to physically get out there and draw a line in the sand—"

"You mean a line in the water?" quipped Ryan.

"This is a joke to you?" Callie glared at him.

Haven stepped in. "I think we all recognize the gravity of the situation. That's why we're here. Let's not fight among ourselves. Callie makes a good point. And so does Ryan. There's no reason we can't fight this on more than one front. Ryan, see if you can find someone to dive down there and get us some underwater footage.

"Callie, call our contacts in the boating community. If we can pull together a flotilla, we might be able to force the ships to alter their routes temporarily at least."

Callie pumped her fist. "We can do this," she said.

"I hope you're right," said Haven.

CHAPTER TWENTY-ONE

Eel had no time for reading newspapers. Between the day job and band practice, he barely had time to think. He did make time for a twice-weekly swimming lesson at the YMCA. He signed up on impulse without really examining his motives and discovered a quiet satisfaction in learning to keep his head above water.

When Squid questioned him about it, Eel said he was doing it for their upcoming boat gig, a party for the employees of a thriving computer business. The company's youthful CEO had been impressed by the style and sound of Eel's band at one of the Alki bars and had offered them good money to play for a party cruise.

"You don't have to swim for this gig, you know," said Squid as he packed up his keyboard the night before the party.

"I know. 'S nice to know I could. If the boat sinks."

"Right. As if."

"Hey. You never know."

The next day they loaded their equipment in the van, drove across the bridge, and got to the pier downtown with time to spare. Eyeing the party boat, Duggan said, "I thought it would be bigger."

"It's plenty big. The guy told me there'll be three hundred people at this thing," said Squid.

Duggan shrugged. "Looks small."

"That's only because it's next to the ferry. You'll see. It's not that small inside."

"How do you know?"

"I saw the pictures."

"Pictures lie."

"Come on, let's get this stuff on board," said Eel.

"I hope I don't get seasick," said Duggan, pulling pieces of his drum kit from the back of the van.

Eel looked past him at the people milling by the ferry dock. A tall guy in the crowd turned and met his eye and nodded in recognition. "Shit," Eel muttered.

"What's the matter?" asked Squid.

"Guy I don't want to talk to."

"Well, come on then."

Eel didn't move. "You go on. I'll be there in a minute."

Eel saw Haven turn and say something to his companions. Then he turned back and started walking toward Eel, who straightened up, watching the way Haven moved through the crowd. In the golden sunshine of late afternoon, Haven's broad shoulders, thick blonde hair, and strong chin set him apart from the disheveled passengers waiting for the ferry. As Haven drew closer, Eel noticed a light in his eyes and wondered what reason he could possibly have for coming over. Wasn't it enough that he had Callie back? Did he need to gloat?

"It's Eel, right?" Haven held out his hand. Eel slowly met it with his own.

"Yeah. And you're... Haven." It wasn't a question, but Haven nodded and smiled in a friendly way that made Eel doubt the gloat motive.

"I saw you over here. I just thought we should meet."

"Huh."

"I know how much you mean to Callie," Haven continued.

Eel stared at him uncertainly.

"Are you here for the protest?" Haven asked.

"The what?"

Haven registered this. If he was disappointed, he didn't let it show. "The cruise ship protest. We're trying to save the kelp forest."

"The what?" Eel said again.

This time Haven frowned. "It's a rare and important habitat that's threatened by the cruise ships that visit Seattle."

"Oh. Yeah." Eel tilted his head. "Kelp's a plant, right?"

"Right. A really important one. But... I don't have time to tell you about it now. Here, read this. It'll tell you what we're fighting for."

Eel accepted the pamphlet and slipped it in his back pocket.

The two men faced each other for a brief, wordless moment. Just as Haven seemed about to go back to his group, Eel roused himself to say, "Is she doin' all right?"

"Callie?"

Eel nodded.

Haven's expression shifted slightly. "She's working really hard on this kelp fight. Sea otters depend on kelp, you know. And the kelp depends on the sea otters. It's a beautiful kind of symbiosis."

Eel wasn't about to ask what that meant. "As long as she's happy."

"I wouldn't say she's happy."

"Whose fault is that?"

"I don't know. Callie doesn't confide in me." He paused. "She never did, really." He started to turn away.

"You're the one she deserves," Eel said.

Haven froze. "I'm not the one she wants."

Eel couldn't summon a reply. Haven looked him steadily in the eye and said, "You should talk to her." Then he turned and walked back to his group, while Eel remained locked in place, his mind racing.

He peered at the crowd, trying to spot a halo of blonde hair. Even if she were over there, he couldn't talk to her now anyway. She'd be in protest mode, and he didn't want to mess with that. He was sick of protests and causes. He just wanted to play his music.

He turned away resolutely and carried his equipment onto the boat. After he reached the deck where the band was set up, he looked back toward the pier. Haven's group appeared to be breaking up. He still couldn't see Callie anywhere.

"Who was that guy?" Squid asked.

"Callie's boyfriend."

Squid raised his eyebrows. "You know him?"

"No."

Squid looked down at the pier and chuckled.

"What?" Eel asked.

"There's a guy down there dressed up like seaweed. Dude's got full-body dreadlocks." Squid grinned. "Looks like they're all going cruising too."

Eel put his guitar down and walked over to watch the protesters. They were dividing up and getting into smaller boats. Some held posters.

"Kind of an unusual place for a protest," said Squid.

Eel gripped the railing tighter. She was stepping into one of the boats. The bobbing motion of the waves and the dazzling light on the water made his head spin with memories of being in a small boat with her.

"Are you okay, man? Seasick?" Squid looked at him cautiously.

Eel swallowed carefully. "It's her."

Squid looked down at the boats. After a minute he said, "What do you suppose they're doing, man? Seems kinda late to be headin' out."

"We're headin' out."

"Yeah, but this is a party boat, man. We're just gonna sail around in a circle. Those guys... I mean, what's up with Seaweed Man? Who's gonna read their posters in the dark?"

Eel turned away. "Don't ask me."

Squid watched him walk away and said, "Hey. What's that thing in your pocket?"

Eel pulled out the pamphlet Haven had handed him and passed it to Squid. "Knock yourself out."

"Help The Kelp," Squid read aloud. "Huh." He read the pamphlet while Eel played his unplugged guitar.

Rob and Duggan came up from below. "The guests are starting to arrive," Duggan said. "You guys should check out the buffet table. Beaucoup shrimp."

Squid looked up. "Maybe later." When he'd finished reading the flyer, he looked at Eel and said, "Do we know where this boat's going?"

Eel shrugged.

Squid waved the flyer at him. "Cause, according to this, those people in the little boats? Callie's people? They're going out to block ships from running over some seaweed."

"Seaweed?"

"Yeah. Kelp."

"Right. He told me. Help the Kelp. Whatever."

"Yeah, well, they're going out there to make like a blockade with their little boats, and we're going out there to sail around, and..." he shrugged. "Hope we don't run into them."

"Why would we?"

"Cause it'll be dark later, and, you know. This is a big boat. They're little boats."

"They must know what they're doing. That guy, Haven, he knows what he's doing."

Squid stared across the water at the motley armada heading out into the Sound. They were mostly small pleasure boats, along with a few kayaks, and a couple of sailboats. Some flew black Jolly Roger flags. Others sailed under Whole Earth pennants. "Says in the flyer that anyone with a boat can join in. They're doing it in shifts. Keepin' a twenty-four hour blockade going. Kinda cool."

Eel kept his head down, fiddling with his amp. A low thrumming sound coincided with a slight shudder on the deck.

"Here we go," said Squid.

From below, an increasing buzz of conversation floated up the stairwell. As the boat turned toward the setting sun, Duggan sat down behind his drums and Rob picked up his bass. Eel played the opening riff to one of their instrumentals, and Squid joined in on the keyboard. The temperature cooled as they got away from the pier. Eel breathed a little easier once he was playing.

Drawn by the sound of the music, the party guests found their way onto the deck and leaned against the railing to watch the sun setting on the water, while the small boats in the flotilla headed off to the north.

Down on the water, leading the flotilla, Callie stared out at the sea. In the two weeks since they had begun guarding the kelp forest, they had encountered dozens of smaller boats, and a few Argosy tour boats. So far all the pilots had accepted the blockade's position and rerouted their crafts around it. Callie and many of the kelp team had been jubilant at first, but Haven remained cautious. He reminded Callie that they had yet to face any of the really huge cruise ships.

"It's only a matter of time, Callie. The season is far from over. We've seen dozens of them going by at a distance. When the traffic picks up and the channel gets crowded, we have to be prepared for one of the monsters to steam too close," he had said.

Callie squinted at the bobbing ring of boats stationed around the edge of the underwater forest site. There were close to twenty boats this night, each lit up with strings of lights and larger beacons to ensure that no ship could fail to see them. But as the darkness deepened, Callie was struck by how small and insignificant their twinkling lights appeared under the vast canopy of sky. Would someone on a cruise ship as big as a city block even notice them? And what would they do if a ship didn't stop?

The local news outlets had given the flotilla scant coverage the first few days of the blockade. Without any obvious dramatic conflict, the story didn't hold the attention of the city's reporters, who had more gripping stories to cover.

Callie fumed silently in the boat, wishing there were some way she could make people see what they were fighting for. They'd managed to post a few underwater photos on the internet, but the newspapers didn't use them, and the TV coverage had offered only a few seconds of footage of the blockade boats and one short sound bite from Haven.

She worried they wouldn't secure legal protection for the site before the volunteers tired of the long nights out on the Sound. Right now there were plenty of students available and willing to pull all-nighters for the cause. If the effort continued into September, they would lose a lot of volunteers to school. The cooler nights and approaching rainy season would discourage others.

For now, the volunteers were in high spirits. The blockade at times almost resembled a floating party, although Callie insisted they not play music because she wanted to be able to hear approaching boats. But on this night she was troubled by the sound of distant music that seemed hauntingly familiar.

She was leaning out over the bow of the boat, straining to hear a melody that teased her ear, rising and falling with the gentle slap of the waves on the boat's hull, when Haven came up behind her and said, "I saw your friend tonight."

Callie turned with a puzzled look. "Who?"

"Your friend. Eel."

Callie's mouth fell open. "What do you mean, you saw him? Where?"

"He was at the pier. Just before we left. I went over to introduce myself. It seemed like a good opportunity." Haven looked at her carefully. She was frowning at the sea.

"Did he want to volunteer?"

"It looked like he was doing something on one of the tour boats."

Callie shook her head and leaned back over the rail. "It doesn't matter." She pinched her lips together as if to keep words from spilling out.

"Have you seen him since the trial?" Haven asked.

"No. He doesn't want to see me. He thinks I belong with you."

Haven smiled ruefully. "Do you?"

Callie sighed. She tilted her chin toward the stars and said, "I'm not sure I belong with anyone. You deserve someone better than me."

"There's no one better than you."

She shook her head impatiently. "Don't be ridiculous. There's a million girls better than me."

"I don't think so."

"Okay. Maybe a hundred thousand. But that's plenty. You just have to get out there and look for them. I can't find 'em for you."

Haven started to reply, but stopped short as he caught sight of something behind Callie. Seeing the look in his eyes, she whipped around and gasped.

It loomed like a black mountain, edged with tiny lights. It was close and getting closer much too quickly.

When the band finished playing a slow blues number that allowed guests who couldn't dance to shuffle cautiously around the deck without fear of embarrassment, Duggan looked up from his drums and exclaimed, "Holy shit!"

Eel turned and felt it like a kick in his gut. The cruise ship towered over them in the night like some giant's castle, dark and menacing.

"Hey, do you think they see those small boats down there?" Squid had gone over to the railing and was peering across the water at the blockade boats floating about fifty yards ahead, directly in the path of the oncoming cruise ship.

Eel didn't stop to answer. He put down his guitar and raced into the ship's cabin to tell the captain to radio the cruise ship and warn them of the small boats. The seconds crawled while the captain made the call, and Eel's heart hammered with cold fear. From the window of the cabin, he could see the cruise ship bearing down on the tiny boats with the implacable force of a glacier, slow and deadly.

The captain looked up from the phone. "It's all right. They've agreed to reduce their speed to give the boats time to get out of the way."

Eel grunted in frustration. "That's not gonna work. They're not gonna get out of the way. That's the whole point."

The captain frowned slightly. "I'm sorry. Did I miss something? I thought you wanted me to ask the ship for time so they could clear out. You want the cruise ship to alter its course?"

"Yes. They have to," Eel said.

The captain looked at him sternly. "Young man, you don't ask a one hundred thousand ton cruise ship to turn around without a damned good reason."

"The reason is those boats are trying to protect a habitat thing, for seaweed—kelp—that's what it is. Special kelp that helps otters and things, and the people in those boats have got lawyers working to make it all legal, and if that ship hurts them there'll be trouble, big trouble for them. Like—bad press—really bad press, and—"

The captain held up his hand. "All right, all right. Let me see what I can do." He picked up the phone again, and Eel paced anxiously while the captain spoke with the cruise ship.

After several more minutes, the captain said, "I see. Yes. I'll tell him."

He turned back to Eel and said, "The captain is sympathetic, but he says he can't alter the course of the ship without compelling evidence. Their routes are carefully mapped and he says there's nothing on their charts to indicate anything such as you describe. There are thousands of people on that ship who've paid a lot of money for the experience, and the company has a responsibility to those passengers." He gave Eel a measured look. "Unless there's something your friends can do to persuade the captain that this is a matter of life and death, they're going to have to move."

Eel frowned. "They're not going to move. He can't just run over them."

The captain shook his head. "He won't have to. He's called the Coast Guard. They're on the way. They'll arrest your friends and impound their boats unless they move out of the way."

Eel glared at the floor for a few seconds. Then he muttered, "Maybe there's something I can do."

He sprinted out of the room and bounded down the stairs. He picked up his guitar and strapped it on and cranked up the volume.

"Are we playing now?" asked Squid.

"No. Just me." Eel faced the flickering circle of lights that bobbed around the dark center where the kelp forest grew. He played the first note of "Shipwrecked" and listened as if measuring its sustain across the water. He turned the amp up as far as it would go and began to play the song.

Everyone on the boat stopped talking as the notes rose from his guitar, and the darkness filled with rhythm and melody, soaring above the water, screaming in the air.

He played through one verse of the song, and when he came to the end a few people clapped tentatively, until he yelled, "Shut up! It's not working!"

Quickly, he played the opening lines of "Blood on the Water," hammering the notes as if he were building a bridge across the empty space between himself and the boat where he knew Callie was listening.

As he began the haunting refrain, the notes leapt from his fingers like sparks of fire, and a murmur rose from the guests lining the railing on the boat. They were staring at the sea inside the blockade, and when Eel looked up, he broke into a wide grin.

There, in the once-dark circle of seawater, the leaves of kelp were glowing with light, pulsing in time to the music. And, as Eel kept playing, a wide shaft of green radiance rose from the kelp and shot high above the flotilla like some primeval klieg light. The light extended deep beneath the surface, lighting up the kelp forest for several meters. The guests oohed with delight when, from the middle of the shining kelp leaves, several otters poked their heads up sleepily as if wondering who or what had disturbed their rest.

A loud cheer rose from the blockade boats. Eel kept playing the song, afraid to stop until some assurance had been received from the cruise ship. He looked up to the bridge, where the captain was staring out at the light show and talking on the phone.

Finally, after another couple of times through the song, the captain came down from the bridge and told Eel, "They're changing their course to avoid the area."

Relief surged through Eel's body, but he still kept playing until they could see the cruise ship backing off. When he let the last note ring, he looked out at the blockade boats. There was an instant of silence before a huge cheer erupted from all the boats.

Drenched in sweat, Eel sat down on his amp. Squid came up to him and slapped him on the back. "That was the most amazing thing I've ever seen. You're awesome man! You got the green mojo workin'!"

Eel grabbed Squid's sleeve and pulled him closer. "Don't say anything to anyone about it," he said.

"What do you mean, man? Everybody saw it. You can't hush something like that up. It was incredible. You're gonna be famous."

"Shhh," Eel whispered furiously. "I don't want to be famous for being a freak. Just don't talk about it. If anyone asks what happened, or how it happened, just say you don't know. People can think what they want. But don't tell them it was me. It wasn't me. It was the music. Coulda been anyone playin' it."

Squid shook his head. "I don't get it. You just did this amazing thing—you saved the day, man. You should be happy."

"Yeah. Sure. I'm happy. Long as Callie's happy."

"Are you kidding? She's gonna be all over you! You're the hero."

"No, I'm not. I just... it was just some kind of freak thing. We'll never know how it happened."

"Yes we will. It was you—"

"Shut up. I mean it. I don't want any of you talking about this to anyone. If anyone asks, you just say you don't know. It's a mystery. Got it? Life is full of mysteries."

Squid kept shaking his head. "Okay. It's a mystery. Nothin' to do with you. Mister Mystery."

"Shut up."

Callie stood in the boat staring at the fading kelp lights, her heart beating wildly. When the first notes of "Blood on the Water" came soaring into the night, she had felt a spasm of anger at Eel for playing her song without asking her permission. But her anger had vanished in breathless wonder when the kelp began to throb with light. And when she thought the night couldn't get any more amazing, she'd seen the otters stirring in the center of it all like some kind of miraculous mirage.

Now as night reclaimed the scene and the cruise ship veered away, she stared across the dark water at the boat that carried the man she loved. It was beginning to turn toward the harbor. In another few minutes it would be out of sight. Without another thought, she stood up, climbed to the edge of the boat, and dove in the water.

CHAPTER TWENTY-TWO

"Man overboard!"

"It's a woman!"

"Woman overboard!"

Eel heard the cries before he saw her. In a searing flash of clarity, he tore off his leather jacket, leapt over the railing and plunged into the frigid water.

He bobbed to the surface spluttering, but kicking confidently, and looked around for Callie. She was treading water a few yards from him, her pale hair floating about her head like a shining veil.

"Are you crazy?" she cried. "You can't swim, remember?"

Eel smiled and started doing the breaststroke toward her. She stared in disbelief. When he reached her, he wrapped his arms around her and pulled her close, and they started sinking. She kicked free of him and said, "Wait a minute! You've got some explaining to do."

"Ah come on, Callie. I'm here, aren't I? What more do you want?"

Something in his eyes cut through all the anger and unhappiness she'd been feeling since the day of the trial. She launched herself into his arms, knocking him backwards. They both went under, and he kissed her, and she held him tight, until they both felt the need for oxygen and kicked to the surface again.

"Hey! Are you guys drowning or what?" Squid was peering at them over the railing of the boat.

"Or what," yelled Callie.

"Seriously, you want us to pick you up, or are you planning to swim home?" Squid asked.

"We should get in the boat," Eel whispered.

"Yeah," said Callie softly, burying her face in his neck. "I've missed you so much," she murmured.

He said nothing, but held her tighter as they waited for the rescue crew to reach them. Once they were on the boat, they looked at each other cautiously.

After the crew and the band and the rest of the onlookers had retreated, and Callie and Eel were alone on the deck, she said, "I went to look for you, and you'd moved away. Why didn't you tell me?"

Eel reached for her hand and held it.

"There were things I had to do. Some things I had to... I didn't know if you—"

"You should have told me. You should have asked me what I wanted. Why did you run off like that after the trial?"

"You're the one who ran off and almost got yourself drowned without telling me, remember?"

"Don't change the subject."

"I'm not. There were things—I learned some things about myself that I didn't know if you could accept."

"Like what? Will you please tell me what's going on? How did you do that tonight? It was you, wasn't it? You made the kelp glow. That was like—"

"Magic. That's the word you're lookin' for. And I don't know. Maybe it was me. But maybe it was you."

"What do you mean?"

"I mean, it didn't work when I played my song. Then I thought, maybe it wants your music. You bein' a sireen and all."

"What? Who told you I was a sireen?"

"Your granddad."

"When did you talk to him?"

"I didn't. Your sisters told me about him and all that mermaid stuff while you were gone. When you left me alone to go off and find Puki by yourself." He paused. "When you didn't trust me."

"I trust you." She hesitated. "I just thought that I had to be alone for it to work."

"And by 'it' you mean?"

Her lips twisted in a sheepish grin. "My magic. Or whatever." She laughed softly. "We're pretty funny, huh?"

He shrugged. "I guess."

She looked at him steadily. "So, what did you do? How did you do that?"

"That's what I'm trying to tell you. Why I had to go away. After Fergus told me about my dad, I didn't think it was right for me to be with you, no matter how much I wanted to be."

"What about your dad? I thought you never knew him."

"I didn't. But Fergus has this idea that my dad was a Green Man, like him. So he took me into the woods, up there," he pointed toward the Olympics. "And we did some experiments. And, long story short, I guess he was right."

"Did you find your father?"

"Nah. Not sure I want to. Still can't believe he was such a bastard to my mom. Probably better not to meet him. Might have to deck him."

"But, does this mean that you're...?"

"I don't know what it means. That's the big question, innit? Fergus says I'm still mortal, probably." He snorted softly. "He told me to practice my magic, like working out at the gym. So. Been doin' that. That's how I found out I could do the glow thing. I didn't know if it would work underwater. I've only ever done it at home on a few plants. But seemed like tonight was a good time to try."

"And it's your music that makes it work?"

"On land anyway. Maybe in the water it's yours."

"So it's both. Maybe that's why we're meant to be together." Callie's face shone.

He shook his head and said, "That's just it. There's nothing wrong with you. You can have a normal life—a good life—with... Haven." Eel cleared his throat. "That's why I went away. Because it's the right thing. For you."

Callie threw her hands up in the air and said, "Would you cut that out? How many times do I have to say this? I want to be with you. You and me. That's what I want."

"Callie. You don't know how bad it can get. When Alice fell in love with Fergus, her whole life fell apart."

"She seems happy now."

"Yeah, well. He's human now, I guess. As human as he's going to be anyway."

Callie studied him in the darkness. The moonlight gleamed on his wet hair and the planes of his cheekbones. His eyes were hooded in shadow. "So..." she said, thoughtfully. "You're not sure if you're human anymore."

"Right. I don't know. Maybe I could find my dad and ask him, but I'm not doin' that."

"But he could be out there? Now? In the Olympic Forest?"

"That's what we think. That's why I can tap into some kind of magical vein or something. Fergus says it's my family tree."

Callie let out a whoop of laughter. "This is soooo great! I've always been the weird one in my family, but you've got me beat! I love it!"

Eel shook his head again. "You don't get it. That's why I can't be with you. You deserve someone you can have a normal life with. What if you want kids?"

"Alice has a kid."

"Yeah but, the jury's still out on that."

"What do you mean?"

Eel glanced up at the stars. "Fergus says she's gonna be a regular kid, but I don't know. He was still a Green Man when she was... you know... planted."

Callie grinned at him. "You are so funny. Do you think I care about normal? Around here we say normal is what you make it."

Eel took a deep breath and stared out at the Sound. Ahead of them, the twinkling skyline of Seattle was getting closer, the reflections rippling in the dark harbor.

He said softly, "So. You want to make 'normal' with me?"

"Anytime. Anyplace."

He reached for her hand. "Maybe we should start on dry land."

"Oh, what fun would that be?"

"Could be magic."

She looked into his eyes. "It already is."

EPILOGUE

Initially, after video footage captured by phones on the cruise ship went viral, the waters surrounding the kelp site were crowded with scientists, activists, and journalists from all over the world. The burst of media attention helped Haven's Sound Sense secure long-sought legal protections for the Puget Sound marine environment, and The Sounding received a grant to expand their sea otter program, enabling them to acquire another orphaned sea otter. Ollie's whiskered face can be seen on buses and brochures all over Seattle.

Callie and Eel coped with a loss of privacy after grainy photos of them embracing in the dark waters of the Sound found their way onto social media, but such celebrity is short-lived. By the time the winter rains settled in, the flotilla was a footnote in local history.

To save money needed to pay off their fines, Callie and Eel decided to share a small rental house in Alki. The band practices in the basement.

They both still work their day jobs. On their days off they've been taking scuba lessons; they haven't given up on finding Puki.

The approach of spring promises new opportunities: Callie's been offered a summer internship with an otter conservation program in Monterey. Eel plans to return to the Bay area to work on his Green Man skills with Fergus.

According to Fergus, there may not be much money in it, but there's unlimited growth potential.

The End

ABOUT THE AUTHOR

Constance Harper Sprague was born in Erie, Pennsylvania, a quiet under-the-radar city with no illusions about itself. She continues to saunter to the beat of a different drummer in the Washington, D.C., area, where she remains a closet whistler, a lifelong daydreamer, and a competent roller skater. She is the author of a half dozen novels, most of them bearing little relation to reality.

ALSO BY CONSTANCE SPRAGUE

**Alice and The Green Man
(Restored Edition)**
CreateSpace 2013

Alice Owens meets the love of her life when a mysterious, immortal Green Man arrives to help protect the garden she planted on an abandoned lot threatened by encroaching development. The Green Man casts a magical spell that sets off a firestorm of media attention, and Alice must risk everything she holds dear. *Alice and The Green Man* is a fairytale for the green at heart.

The Greening
Silver Beech Press 2013, 2015

Book One: At The Root
Book Two: In The Wave
Book Three: On The Wing

In this alt-fantasy series, an eco-terrorist group unwittingly releases toxic magic on Earth, causing worldwide chaos. As Shiloh Carter and her daughter Eva fight to restore order, they uncover family secrets and discover magic powers of their own. When Destiny comes calling, they join forces with a ragtag crew of not-quite superheroes for the final battle to save the world from fiery Armageddon.

http://constancesprague.com